I

PERISCOPE ZERO

A WWI U-BOAT THRILLER

EK-2 PUBLISHING

Your Satisfaction Is Our Goal!

Dear Readers,

First, we would like to thank you for purchasing this book. Our goal is to inspire readers from all over the world with our historical and military novels and biographies.
We are a family business, and our team thrives to offer you a unique reading experience and of course, we want to increase our quality with each book published.
We are grateful for your feedback as well as ideas about books you may want to read in the future. Your opinion matters to us. Do you have any comments or criticism? Please let us know. Your feedback is of great value to us and of course to our authors as well. Be part of our publishing journey and our EK-2 publishing family. Write to us at:

info@ek2-publishing.com

And now we wish you an entertaining reading experience with this book.

Your EK-2 Publishing Team
The publisher close to its readers

Prolog

Beyond all Hope

The men hung on the rescue net or stretched as far over the railing as they could. But none of them spoke. They were experienced men. Much too experienced, but that was also normal at the beginning of the fourth year of the war.

Nevertheless, despite all the experience, there was still a little hope left. Always! Even if there couldn't be any by all reason. And that's why the men were silent, stared at the dark water surface, tried to penetrate the drifting mist with their eyes; that's why the trawler chugged dangerously close to the mine field sailing less than dead slow.

Suddenly the ship's boy raised his hand. The others froze, looking in the direction the young sailor pointed. Then they all saw it, in the light of the dimmed lamp. First there was only a ghostly appearance in the water, then details emerged from the darkness. Long hair and a beard framing a wide-open mouth apparently still wanting to scream out his disappointment. Somewhere was a choking retching.

Then there was another noise. A call for help. The mate pointed in one direction and the warrant officer, who commanded the trawler as a VP-boat, turned the wheel... because there was always some hope left, even if there really couldn't be any left.

1
Fog over the Sea

Tuesday, January 30, 1917, 40 miles north of Ireland... the third year of the war.

The commander's gaze glided discontentedly across the sea's surface – or at least what he could see of it. It wasn't much. Wafts of mist were floating everywhere over the gray water. Only the tiniest swell moved the Atlantic here at the northern exit of the British ports from the Irish Sea. Theoretically SM U-15 was in a good position to lie in wait for English merchant ships. Theoretically!

"Damn fog, in this weather we won't see a merchantman until she's almost running us over."

Lieutenant Commander Erwin Müller turned his attention to his 2nd Watch Officer, short form: IIWO.

"If it's a single vessel, it's probably a neutral anyway, and we aren't allowed to attack." The old man shrugged his shoulders. "Of course, they transport all food and ammunition to the Limeys, but they're neutral after all, the Americans first."

"Well, Herr Kaleun?"

"So we'll see that we catch a British convoy. At least we can attack them without warning."

"And every armed merchant ship, right?"

Müller suppressed the urge to roll his eyes. "Of course, we just have to see the cannon at first in this fog."

Sub-Lieutenant Andreas Rader, the IIWO, pondered for a moment. "Right again."

"Well, I'm glad we agree." The old man pulled his pocket watch out of the U-boat pack and studied the clock face. "About two hours till sunrise. When you see the first light, give morning alarm, but then dive. If the fog remains we'll hear the Englishmen with the hydrophone rather than spotting them."

"Yes, Herr Kaleun!"

"Very well then, I'll be below and take a nap." Müller squeezed his way through the lookouts and disappeared through the tower hatch.

In the control room he was once more surrounded by the cramped world of the submarine, but at four in the morning it was a little calmer than usual even in this godforsaken iron tube. A little, not much. Of course, the watches went on around the clock and the engines had to run permanently as well.

Lieutenant Commander Müller nodded to the con mate before disappearing into his tiny cabin. Only when he had closed the curtain did he drop in his chair in front of the miniscule desk and took a deep breath. Rader was inexperienced, a red brat straight from the textbook – if there was such a thing as a textbook for red brats. Müller suspected there had to be one. There was a rule book for virtually everything in Germany. He grinned weary. No, that was unfair, he admitted to himself. Rader was young, fresh from officer training and had served previously his one and only time at sea on a training ship. The training ships produced good soldiers, but they couldn't produce good naval officers out of nothing. That called for experience and now, in the third year of the war, nobody had the time to wait for young men to gather that experience. The Imperial German Navy put new boats into service every month. The High Seas Fleet grew steadily and now there were also naval field battalions, naval base battalions, naval artillery battalions and God knew what else. Not only the men for all these units had to come from somewhere, but also the officers to lead them. Officers like Andreas Rader were everywhere. Too young, too quickly pulled up in the greenhouse. He'd learn his trade. If the war would let him stay alive long enough to learn.

U-15 was an old boat and Lieutenant Commander Müller was aware of that. Old ... not so much by years, she had been launched in 1909, just eight years ago, but old in the terms of a war that already had left far behind everything anyone could have imagined before. New type U-93 submarines had six tubes and a total of 22 tin fishes onboard, Müller's U-15 had just four tubes and if the torpedoes in them were fired, he had only two in spare. Hardly an arsenal to cause much damage on a convoy but the

German Empire could not afford to fight the war at sea without the older subs despite their lower combat value. Germany had to end the war as quickly as possible. Already now, civilians were dying at home from malnutrition, a result of the British starvation blockade. Germany was still able to hang on, but not forever. And since the war had become entrenched on land, Germany's only hope was to starve the English by a blockade, just as they starved the Germans. Müller thought of the sealed orders in his safe. Of course, he hadn't read them yet, he had orders to open them on the morning of February 1st, but just as naturally he already knew what the orders included. Everyone in the U-boat weapon knew it, it had been only a matter of time after all: Germany would resume the unrestricted submarine warfare. That meant more submarines, and of course the newer and bigger submarines would get the better sailors. Which brought him back to Rader. Somehow he had to figure out how to make the man a useful watch officer … because once the dance would really begin, he needed to rely on each man in his crew. The English and especially their American friends on the other side of the Atlantic would not accept a blockade of England without resistance.

*

On the tower Andreas Rader tried to peek through the whirling veils of fog. Wasn't that damn pea souper getting a little lighter? But whenever he tried to spot something in a particular direction, dense wafts of mist would again pass through his vision. Slowly, only making two knots, the boat crept through the calm sea, but the low speed promised only a deceptive safety and Rader was fully aware of that. If a freighter were to come out of the fog now, she would run over the U-boat in less than half a minute. Two knots made every evasive maneuver hopelessly slow. Half a minute could barely be enough to get away in that situation, but certainly it was not enough to dive into the safe depth. And if such a freighter should be a Limey, he could even punch them right in the face with his cannon.

Only when finally something appeared out of the fog, it was not a big merchantman.

"Boat, one Dez on starboard!"

Rader spun around and raised his binoculars. Then he let them sink again. It was really just a boat. A lonely lifeboat. He could see seven men, but none of them stood up or waved. They must have been dead for days, perhaps weeks, forgotten by the world of the living. Still, Rader startled briefly. Something was wrong. There was something very wrong with this lonely lifeboat. He bent over the speaking tube.

"Engines stop. Hard starboard. Commander on the tower, please."

The low chugging of the machines had already died when he heard the confirmation of his orders from below. Driven by the remaining speed, the bow swung around a little, closer to the floating boat. Now Rader could see it better. Seven men and all wore uniforms!

Behind him, the skipper climbed out of the hatch, the cap as always boldly crooked on his skull. "What do we have?"

The sub-lieutenant reported: "Lifeboat, Herr Kaleun!"

Müller considered the discovery of his IIWO for a moment, then he nodded.

"Good thinking! Call for the bosun, he shall secure the boat! I want to have a closer look."

A few minutes later the boat was safely moored to the starboard saddle tank of U-15. Lieutenant Commander Müller threw a glance up to the watch on the tower, but Sub-Lieutenant Rader and his lookouts kept their eyes on their sectors and paid no attention to the distraction on the long foredeck. Satisfied, Müller turned away and watched the lifeboat. Seven men, and now that they were so close, he could see that they could not be dead for long. Probably died of thirst. The idea of languishing on an ocean full of water sent a shiver down his spine, but he managed to keep a detached expression. His men were watching him.

"They all have the same cap ribbon."

Jäger, the bosun, stepped beside him. "Except for the officer."

"That's right, except for the officer." The lieutenant commander nodded quietly. The officer was still holding his arm on the tiller. He could clearly see the two wavy stripes on the sleeve. A British reserve officer. The Limeys had to have thousands of them. An island people, they certainly didn't run out of sea-experienced officers.

He nodded. "Bring the men aboard. I want the radio operator to search them, and I want to see everything he finds."

"And then what?"

"Then we'll put them to rest decently and make a log entry." The old man hesitated. "Maybe they have dog tags. Somebody's waiting for them somewhere."

"And the boat?"

Müller blinked. "Search it, then sink it."

"Yes, Herr Kaleun!"

The commander stretched out a little and looked around. They still had time until sunrise, but the fog was too dense to see further than maybe 100 meters. Goddamn fog, one never knew what the hell was in it!

2
A Riddle

Tuesday, 30 January 1917, 40 miles north of Ireland ...

Radio operators were a rare breed, so to speak. Many civilian ships still had no radios, and even those that had were limited in range. Of course warships and submarines had radio stations, but naturally they were only useful if one was close enough to a coast where a friendly radio station could pick up the messages and forward them, or if other ships did that. Normally, German submarines did not operate within the range of friendly radio stations, and even the few who did occasionally, like U-15, kept radio silence so as not to tell the enemy where they were lurking. Theoretically, radio operators on the emperor's submarines did not have much to radio and therefore he was not only assigned with operating the radio, but furthermore had the secondary task of a paramedic, because there was certainly no doctor on a submarine. In practice, however, there was already a lot to do, of course, because the English and the neutrals radioed diligently and, moreover, the Germans were dependent on the British weather reports. The German weather report could not be transmitted to the operational areas of the U-boats. Thus, Otto Heidkamp was in fact a very busy man.

The radio operator turned his cap unsteadily in his hands. "You know, Herr Kaleun, I ain't no doctor, but I guess they have been dead at most for four or five days. Died of thirst, by the looks of it."

The commander thoughtfully stroked his beard. "All dead for the same amount of time?"

"No, I think the lieutenant was the last one kicking it." Heidkamp shook himself involuntarily. "Must have been sitting at the tiller by the time the others were already kaputt."

"So nobody was wounded in the first place?"

"Nah, they were all fine when they got in that cockleshell."

"That fits in with what the bosun says. The boat was fine, too. Only the emergency provisions were missing."

"It is strange if you ask me. The bosun told me that the boat was coated in grey?"

Müller nodded. Heidkamp spoke in a strong Berlin dialect and often appeared as if butter would not melt in his mouth, but the "sparks", as the submariners called their radio operator, rarely missed a detail.

"Yes, grey. Like a warship."

The two men looked at each other, then Heidkamp bowed assent. "We ain't caught no SOS from any man o' war and we've been around here for a week."

"That's right. So the vessel sank before anyone could radio for help, or for some other reason it didn't radio when it sank. Maybe the power died away?"

"How far can a cockleshell like this go in a week?" Heidkamp shrugged his shoulders. "Most big warships nowadays have emergency equipment with batteries with a range of 20 to 30 miles."

"Yeah, it's all a little mysterious, isn't it?" Müller grimaced. "Anything the men had with them?"

"Wallets. One had a pay book with him, dog tags and some photos and letters."

"Anything interesting?"

"Dunno, maybe you'll take a look at it yourself. If you ask me, they've been to New York."

"New York? What makes you think that, Heidkamp?"

"The Statue of Liberty!"

Müller blinked. "Is it in one of the pictures?"

"A Photo. It shows one of the men and a woman with the Statue of Liberty in the background for sure."

"Bring me all the stuff, then we'll pack it all up. Let the brass at home take care of it."

"Yes, Herr Kaleun!" Heidkamp made a face. "I take care of the dead. We sure have no cloth, but a couple of blankets will do."

"Thank you, Heidkamp."

After the radio operator left, Müller leaned back. It was a riddle, but the more important question at the moment was whether it was a riddle he had to solve here and now. Obviously, a British warship had gone down without sending any distress call. Such things happened from time to time. Maybe even one of their own U-boats had hit that vessel. Müller's task was to sink merchant ships, and so far the success of this patrol was rather meager. Still, New York and the English warship ... how did those fit together? The Americans were not as neutral as they pretended, but when a British warship left New York, it had escorted a convoy. Did that mean that a fellow submarine had already salted Müller's hunting grounds? Or did it rather mean that the next convoy would come through here as well? Somewhere the Limeys had to sneak through, after all, they could not land millions of tons of freight on Ireland's west coast. As things stood in Ireland, then the Irish would do the work for the Germans and blow up as much material as they could. So their only option was reaching the Irish Sea and then sail through to Liverpool. But did the Limeys go for a stroll closer to the Irish coast or the Scottish coast? If Müller now backed the wrong horse, then at some point he would run out of gasoline and then he could cart his torpedoes back home again.

Weary, he looked at the track chart on his tiny desk. It was a mystery, and somehow this lifeboat was part of it. A British warship had visited New York. Theoretically the ships of belligerent powers could of course always make for neutral ports and even carry out repairs there, as long as such repairs served the seaworthiness of the ship and not an increase in fighting capabilities. International law made fine distinctions in this aspect. Therefore, the British could, for example, bunker fuel in American ports at any time and even wait for a convoy, as long as they did not do it too long. That was the crux of the matter. Normally a warship had to leave a neutral port within 24 hours at the latest if it was to comply with international law, but of course that time limit was at the discretion of the neutral power that owned the port, and usually many neutral nations allowed 72 hours reasoning that repairs to restore seaworthiness would need a little more time. But American neutrality was one-sided. If a German warship should make a port call to the USA, the Americans would find one reason or another to seize it, while an Englishman could always count on support. Still, just by the mere letters of the law, Lieutenant Commander Müller was sure, the American policy was ironclad.

Only this special case didn't make any sense. The question was not whether the Limeys could enter New York; without doubt, they could. The true question was: why would they? Even if London already knew what was coming – and of course officially Müller knew nothing about it himself, but it was all over town already – there was no need for the British to protect convoys all the way from America. The German U-boats lacked the range to operate on the other side of the Atlantic. So it would be quite good enough to rendezvous the escorts somewhere halfway. Thus if an English warship had been in America, there were only two possible reasons: Either, the Americans had begun now to carry out overhaul work for the Limeys, because the shipyards in England worked of course on full capacity and beyond at the construction of new ships. That would of course be a flagrant violation of all international laws and would make the USA officially a belligerent power, but Müller was not sure whether the Americans even cared about it anymore.

Or, and that would make the whole situation even more complicated, the Limeys had something other than submarines in mind. Maybe a merchant raider or a blockade runner. SMS Möwe was currently out in the Atlantic and SMS Wolf operated in the Indian Ocean after mining the ports of Bombay and Colombo. So Wolf, too, if the raider had set course home, could be located in the Atlantic right now and, as rumor had it shortly before U-15 had put to sea, SMS Seeadler had also set off in December to haunt the enemy's shipping routes. Of course nobody had informed the U-boat commanders about the orders of the raiders and, by the nature of things, these ships operated completely independently. There was no possibility to keep in touch with the homeland since Germany had lost its colonies and thus its last own radio stations outside Europe. So Müller had no idea where the comrades were, but one possibility was that one of them was lurking somewhere in the North Atlantic waiting for his chance to break through into home waters. This would also explain why British warships would roam the American side of the Atlantic. Only if a British cruiser had run into one of the raiders, the Germans would have been brought down but not the English. The ship from which the men in the lifeboat came must have been smaller, or older, as a cruiser but if one of the raiders had sunk a destroyer in the approaches of the Irish Sea, this would be a completely different ballgame here. The Limeys would radio as if there was no tomorrow and try to catch the bold intruder.

It was quiet, way too quiet. Thus, no merchant raider! And according to Müller's orders, U-15 was the only U-boat currently lurking in this area for merchant ships … so, who had sunk an English warship on the way back from America?

The old man pushed the chart aside. He didn't have the faintest idea. Maybe it wasn't his problem … but the nasty feeling remained, something was going on near enough to present them with an ugly surprise at the most inopportune moment.

3
Unrestricted U-boat War

Thursday, 1 February 1917, 45 miles north of Ireland …

The men in the bow compartment did what they always did: they played skat. After all, any war patrol consisted mostly of waiting, and this time it was especially bad. They hung out north of Ireland now for almost a week and a half and as of yet, they had to see as much as a single ship. Nobody even dared to talk about sinking one at all. But naturally, every Hans and Franz considered himself a strategic genius and that's why each knew very well that the commander should have sailed farther north, or lurk somewhere farther out in the open Atlantic or … or … there were different views in the bow compartment about what the old man should have done and what not and of course everyone knew rock solidly that his view was the only one right.

When the loudspeaker cracked, the sailors and machinists looked up in astonishment. A speech? In fact, moments later, the voice of the IWO came out of the tannoy: "Attention for an announcement of the commander!" and a heartbeat later they heard Lieutenant Commander Müller, "Men of U-15, since this morning, February 1, 1917, new orders apply. The German Reich has declared the unrestricted submarine warfare for the waters around England." Müller hesitated for a moment before continuing: "This means that ships can be attacked without warning, even at the risk that they are neutrals. The mere fact that they sail the waters around England can be understood as the transport of embargoed goods. That'll be all for now!"

For a moment silence prevailed in the crammed bow compartment, then diesel machinist Willemann was the first to let the air escape from the lungs whistling: "Unrestricted submarine warfare? Didn't we try this before?"

Electrician mate Hinze nodded. "Two years ago. But they called it off again because it upset the Americans and nobody wanted them to join the war against us. It was bad enough that U-20 sunk the Lusitania back then."

Spontaneously the glances turned to boatswain`s mate Kern, but the burly sailor just shrugged.

"You know what it's like, we stuck in the forward torpedo room. The old man – Schwieger – was the only one who saw anything."

"You must have talked about it after the sinking." Willemann looked at Kern questioningly. But the other sailor just shrugged again. Kern had served on U-20, he had been there when Lieutenant Commander Schwieger had kicked the Lusitania under water and right on the next patrol, the Hesperian, another liner. Of course, Schwieger had torpedoed the Hesperian months after the emperor had already prohibited attacks on liners. But in fact it was the sinking of the Lusitania that stuck to everyone who had served on U-20 like a rotten smell one just could not get rid of. Kern saw the wondering faces around him. "Of course, there's always a lot of talk in the forward room." He hesitated. "We all heard the second explosion. After the tin fish had already hit her, long after that."

"So the Limeys were transporting ammunition on a liner? Then the sinking was justified, wasn't it?"

"And how do you prove that, you brain acrobat?" Kern sent a sourly glance to Hinze. "Everything's on the bottom of the sea, so nobody dives down and looks, do they? Besides, the Limeys have all their liners armed, just like their cargo ships. What do they expect? That we show up and friendly ask for the cargo papers while they paste us?"

"Relax, comrade, so the sinking was fine!" Hinze nodded. "But the Yanks still didn't like it."

Willemann pulled a face. "They won't like it this time either. So we'll probably be at war with them soon. And it doesn't look too good for us anyway."

Kern blinked. "Who knows? Maybe the we stuck already so deep in the shit, it doesn't matter anymore?"

"Who knows?" Willemann nodded. "We will be the last they will tell, won't they?" He grinned. "Neither the emperor, nor

Hindenburg and certainly not our very venerated admiral von Holtzendorff."

Kern drew in air sharply. Willemann was a troublemaker. The man had already held almost every rank from sailor to petty officer and who knows how often he had been degraded again. Only more and more he developed into a dangerous troublemaker. Kern had served in the Imperial Navy long before the war. He knew his stuff. Only things changed and hotheads like Willemann became more common. Something seethed in the bow compartments of the U-boats, the naval barracks and the crew decks of the High Seas Fleet. But it still happened beneath the surface and Adolf Kern was pretty sure that the officers hadn't noticed anything yet. But if ... but if, then a hothead like Willemann could quickly get someone to face a peloton.

Slowly he shook his head. "No, they're not. But we are at war and while we are, we have to do a duty, don't we? We cannot just walk away from a war like this?" He looked at Willemann. What the machinist had hinted did not smell like open mutiny – not yet!

*

Of course, the new orders were discussed in the officers' mess too, even though the officers had to show much more restraint than the simple sailors. Because right now the master had the watch, for a change, all four officers were gathered in the mess. Lieutenant Max Rothe, the IWO, just waved off. "It's about time. The Americans ship endless amounts of ammunition across the pond. Without them, the limeys and frogs would have ran out of steam long ago. Basically the Americans are already at war."

Lieutenant Wilhelm Klempke, the chief engineer, called LI, drew a face as if a stomach ulcer was about to break through. "Yes, but then they'll also ship troops over and our army's already stuck. They already have one and a half French or English division against every German one. What are we going to do if the Americans join them?"

"First the Americans have to cross the Atlantic, which give us the opportunity to shave them when they try."

Andreas Rader blinked. Of course, he was worried. If one was not worried during a war, he had to be really stupid. If the Americans went to war against Germany, and by now this seemed inevitable given the new orders, the imperial U-boats had to try to sink the troop transport vessels before they could reach England.

Rader wasn't good with people. The Navy had made him an officer because he had abitur and understood a thing or two about sailing. But no one knew better than himself that he would never be an officer like the old man. His goal before the war got in the way, had been to study mathematics. Not history or politics. For Andreas Rader, the whole world fell apart into numbers. Nice logical numbers. Only that the numbers no longer looked beautiful and logical should America join the war.

The commander cleared his throat. "Gentlemen, please!"

The IWO implied a bow. "My apologies, Herr Kaleun."

"It's all right." Müller stopped him with a wave of his hand. "Let's put it this way: We have our orders. The orders don't say us how to handle passenger steamers and we all don't want to produce a second Lusitania case, thus, we stay clear of them. We catch a freighter, she goes on out account, and should it be a neutral one, well, it's war after all and if a vessel sails these waters, where else but to England it could be bound?" He sighed. "But first, we have to find those steamers. We're vegging out here and don't see a single ship, and yet this area is supposed to drone from traffic."

"Yeah, it's weird, isn't it?" Klempke pursed his lips.

Rader opened his mouth but already when he started to speak, he regretted it. "They can't just have vanished. Thus, they have to be somewhere else. Logical!"

"Yes, but where, Herr Leutnant?"

"In America, or more likely, on the way from there to here." In front of his inner eye, the numbers began to unite, to form equations and relations. "If, for example, 1,000 ships sail each on their own, they will, after a while, spread out evenly. In other words, every day about the same number of ships would pass the norther approach into the Irish Sea. However, if the English organize convoys, then suddenly only every few days a convoy comes by, because the ships have to wait at the beginning of the voyage for the convoy to be gathered."

Klempke, the engineer, nodded. "That makes sense!"

"Just... where are the convoys, then?" The Lieutenant Commander pondered loudly. "Until now, only the Limeys were organized in convoys, and not even all of them. You think, they introduce a convoy system now throughout?"

The young lieutenant shrugged his shoulders. "That depends on how long they know already, we resume the unrestricted submarine warfare."

"The announcement's is just out today..." Rothe held his breath. "You think...?"

"Let's say three weeks across the Atlantic, two weeks more to organize a convoy, and we haven't seen a ship in nine days. So they must've known what was coming at least 26 days ago. Probably longer."

"That's some strong stuff, Herr Leutnant!" The commander frowned. "That means we wait a few more days, and then the first of many convoys shows up?"

"Two weeks minus x..." Rader turned red. "Sorry, I didn't mean to be arrogant, Herr Kaleun, but I have no idea how much earlier than 26 days ago the English knew what was coming."

Müller raised his eyebrows. "What does that mean?"

"Tomorrow, the day after tomorrow, two weeks at the latest." Rader stared uncertainly into the coffee cup in front of him, avoiding the questioning glances. "If they're not here in two weeks, I'm wrong."

"Why here and not in the south?"

"The cargo ships are slower; they'll stay on the Northern Great Circle as long as possible. For them the southern access is only one to two days at sea more. And most of the sinkings happened in the southern approach so far. The liners on the other hand are fast, they probably run on their own anyway."

"So you make a case for just waiting right here?"

"You're the commander, Herr Kaleun. If you think I'm wrong, please ignore everything I said."

Müller stroked his beard thoughtfully. "You know what? Actually, I think you're right. It would at least explain what we see, or rather don't see."

"But such a convoy, if it exists, won't be the first thing we'll see." Lieutenant Rothe nodded slowly. "Two years ago, the Limeys sent whole packs of cruisers and destroyers to clean the shipping routes of us submarines. Of course, it didn't work. On the contrary. If they started looking around somewhere, we knew something was coming. It was the beginning of the whole convoy malaise, right?"

"I was still IWO on an UC sub at that time, we rather saw the whole story from the sidelines. We were in the mining business back then. Only two years have passed and we all have learned so many new tricks since. We, but also the English, right?"

4
A Lucky Hit

Saturday, February 3, 1917, 40 miles northwest of Ireland …

"Smoke plume, Herr Kaleun!"

"Just one?" Müller raised his eyebrows. "He is alone?"

Lieutenant Rothe approved. "Looks like it, but he's still far away."

"If he's alone, he's balls, I give him that. The Limeys have passed on the news of unrestricted submarine war to ships at sea via all their radio stations … openly to make sure everybody knows what's going on."

The IWO shrugged his shoulders. "It was to be expected. Heidkamp has listened in too."

"All right, so let's be cautious."

"Cautious?"

Müller watched Rothe calmly. "Yes, it feels like there is something in the wind. One alone after the whole world got riled up about the submarine blockade, that stinks! Either she's a very normal English steamer who was just out at sea and now rolls the dice to get home, or maybe she's a neutral who trusts, we will respect his neutrality, or – that would be the last thing we need – the guy's a Q-ship. But no matter what, if we mess with her, the Limeys will know we're lurking here."

It took a moment for the IWO to understand. "You want to let him pass? Because you hope later a whole convoy will follow?"

"Maybe!" Müller observed the distant light gray plume on the horizon. From here it looked more like a thin feather. "Pretty light, isn't it? Could be an oil burner, but then he's got good oil."

"Good oil could mean a warship."

"Right!" The commander came to a decision. "Keep an eye on him. We'll let him come nearer, then we dive and I take a closer look at this bird."

*

The diving maneuver was always a moment of tense nerves. Of course submarines were built to dive, but on the other hand they were still quite a new weapon and complicated machines. The balance of the U-boat, the speed, everything went into the maneuver and if one of the many valves in the hectic might have been closed instead of opened, or opened too wide, if one of the switches was pressed or not pressed, if something suddenly jammed, then anything could happen. The navy had already lost U-boats before the war due to accidents and technical breakdowns, and in the war there had been various losses, because U-boats had to emerge suddenly, although they were hunted by the enemy, or because something had failed. Even in peacetime, when no one shoot at them, the service of the submariners was a dangerous business. Even the youngest Jack Tar was aware of that, and therefore the nerves of everybody aboard were tense during every diving maneuver.

"Take us down to 20 meters." Lieutenant Commander Müller nodded to the LI. "Slow and comfy!"

"Yes, Herr Kaleun."

Klempke turned to the warrant officers. "Dive planes forward ten up, aft fifteen down!" He waited until the depth rudders reached the new position, then he continued: "Blow out cells one, two, seven and eight."

Handwheels were turned and hissing air escaped from the cells. Slowly the bow descended a little, and inside the boat they heard a few waves banging against the conning tower. Then it went quiet. The men in the control room kept their eyes on the depth gauge, slowly the pointer began to move and the water in the glass tube of the measuring unit began to rise.

"Passing ten meters!"

"Secure cells!" Klempke waited a moment, then he continued: "Forward down two, aft zero!"

Again, it took a moment for the bow to straighten up and for the chief engineer to give his next command: "Forward zero, aft zero!"

The boat almost sluggishly aligned itself horizontally. The LI turned to the commander, "Boat at 20 meters!"

"Thank you, LI." Müller looked briefly at the compass. "New course will be two-seven-five, revolutions for two knots!"

Little by little the men relaxed. Of course, there could go always everything go awry on a submarine, but for the moment everything seemed to work. Müller looked around. "IWO, you take over, I'm in the radio room." He grinned. "We just have to wait for that vessel to come to us, we're almost on course."

Heidkamp was already sitting at the hydrophone and turned carefully the handwheel. When the commander stepped next to him, he nodded only marginally. "Got him, Herr Kaleun. Bearing three-five-two."

The commander nodded. Three-five-two, that was almost ahead. That vessel ran right towards them. "What kind of machine does he have?"

"That ain't not easy to say over this distance. Piston machine, but which one?"

Müller was thinking. In principle, piston machines on freighters were always the same, the only difference being whether the boilers were heated with oil or coal. It would have been different if the vessel had had diesel engines, but of course that would have been rare luck – or misfortune, because diesel engines were only used by warships.

"Let's wait and see. If he's close, you might hear pumps."

"This may take some time." Heidkamp frowned. "He must be at least ten miles away."

Müller agreed. Of course, determine a distance from the hydrophone was a mere estimate. There was no way to measure how far away the other ship was, but experienced listeners like Heidkamp could sometimes make surprisingly accurate guesses. "Keep her under observation. We'll approach her up to a mile and see what we got."

"Will do, Herr Kaleun."

The commander returned to the control room and looked around. Everything seemed to run smoothly. Which meant most of the men didn't do anything. There wasn't much to do on a submerged submarine. But of course each of the men still had to be at his post in case the situation changed quickly. The engine watch stood next to their silent aggregates ready in case the boat had to suddenly emerge, the E-mates watched their quietly humming electric motors in case even the slightest irregularity occurred, and in the control room the LI pretended to be bored while in reality he waited for the slightest change of the trim. Even the sailors who waited in the bow compartment fulfilled a function: they were the living ballast during the dive, which could be commanded forward or astern, as well as the muscle support for the machinists, if something stuck or a broken out rivet had to be wedged.

The boat produced some low crackling noises and some of the men lifted their heads, but the LI made a reassuring gesture. "The lady's just sitting down, don't worry."

Müller smiled. The German U-boats had a test depth of 50 meters. Of course they could go deeper, theoretically, but no one dared to even guess how much deeper. 70 meters? Might be. 90? Maybe, who could know? 100? Maybe not! The rising water pressure would begin to compress the steel tube like a tin can. First the rivets would break out, then whole plates would be pressed inwards. The cold water of the Atlantic would break into their little refuge under the sea like a green glassy wall and drown all life in the boat. But 20 meters, that was all right, still a long way from the shipyard guarantee.

"Relax, men. One and a half to two hours till we are close enough to have a good look at him through the periscope."

Little by little everybody was looking for a free place. That was no easy task in a submarine and there were no seats, chairs or benches at all. But submariners were used to such inconveniences. As long as it did not get any worse, the world was fine.

The minutes elapsed in tenacious slowness. Somewhere some of the men were whispering. Silence in the boat wasn't ordered explicitly, but of course the men avoided any unnecessary noise. They were trained that way. 1917 was already the fourth calendar year of war and a relatively large part of the crew had experience. Too much experience, some might say. Allegedly, the human mind can only take so much, but then again, the war did not care at all about human limitations.

Lieutenant Commander Müller leaned at the chart table next to the master and observed his crew: the old, the new, the hard, and those who showed already signs of wear. Like the boat itself. A technical factor. People could break just as easily as machine parts, and in the crowded world of this iron tube with equally fatal consequences. But he wasn't worried. No more than usual anyway. At the moment the situation was still relaxed. How things would be under pressure was of course always a different story.

Finally, after a time that had felt to most of them like an eternity, the radio operator whispered from his little cubbyhole: "I think, he's close enough if you wanna try it now, Herr Kaleun?"

"Thank you, Heidkamp." The old man left the chart table. "Herr Klempke, you heard the man? Periscope depth, if you please!"

The periscope depth of type U-13 submarines, to which U-15 belonged, was five and a half meters, thus just a little less than 15 meters from their present depth. It only took the LI a moment to report that the boat had reached periscope depth. Müller nodded to one of the stokers: "Bring it up!"

He pressed his face against the bead of the periscope. At first he saw nothing at all, then a glassy green shimmer, but before anything could take shape, the head of the periscope broke already through the water surface. Müller's brain automatically registered the details. Swell's more like two rather than three. He quickly turned the "asparagus" into the bearing of the approaching vessel. Two miles, a little more. "Tanker, flies no flag!"

"No flag! Then he's a limey!"

Rothe was right. The British merchant ships did not fly a flag and had orders to ram submarines on sight, which of course had made a war following the provisions of the admiralty laws impossible and was the reason for U-boat attacks without warning. Technically, the English had already broken the cruiser rules years ago. But nobody talked about that!

Müller studied the ship a moment longer. "The angle's too sharp, I can't see his stern, but he's got a gun on the foredeck."

"Then he must be a limey!"

Müller released the handles of the periscope and nodded to the stoker. "Retract!"

The asparagus disappeared again into its shaft with a low grinding sound. The commander nodded. "All right, we can't let a tanker just go! And he's pretty certainly English! Revolutions for one knot, new course will be straight north!"

"Jawohl, Herr Kaleun!"

"IIWO, you take the con. IWO, you launch the torpedo!"

The two officers confirmed. A torpedo was a complicated weapon, basically a small submarine in its own right, only that it did not carry a crew, but a deadly warhead. Still its run depth under the surface had to be set up carefully. Moreover, depending on the distance, a torpedo needed minutes to pick up speed and reach its target. Torpedoes were not fired directly at a ship, but at a point where the target would be at a time the tin fish also needed to reach the very same point. The course was determined by the course of the submarine when the weapon was launched. So everything had to fit together and the IWO had a lot of calculations to perform.

"Flood tubes I and II!"

Lieutenant Rothe threw a few numbers on a piece of paper. "Depth?"

The commander imagined the tanker in his mind. "Let's say four meters. He sails at about ten knots, but we have to make sure. Distance two miles."

The normal procedure would have required two knots, but the ship was running almost straight towards the firing position. "Raise periscope!" Again the old man pressed his head against the eyepiece and took the bearing of the tanker. And a minute later again. Three points, relative to the submarine, that gave the IWO speed and course of the tanker relative to their own and thus the course they had to take when firing the torpedo.

"700 meters!" The old man checked again through the periscope. "Tube I … fire!"

With a hiss, compressed air pushed the torpedo out of the tube, while the LI had already water flowing into the forward trim cells to compensate for the weight loss. Torpedoes weren't just fired. Everything played together like a well-oiled machine. Müller folded the handles up. "Periscope down!"

He waited a moment until the attack optic disappeared into the shaft, then nodded to the IIWO. "Bring us around to zero-nine-five, Herr Leutnant. Revolutions for ten knots!"

The LI quite noisily sucked in a breath. The older U-boats could actually run more than ten knots submerged, but that speed came at the price of draining the batteries in a jiff. Still, Commander Müller ignored the engineer. They did not need to run at full speed submerged for hours on end. Just a few minutes, until ...

"Tanker's changing course, Herr Kaleun!" Heidkamp's warning cut in his thoughts.

"Periscope up!"

He angrily swiveled the asparagus into the vessel's bearing. There he was, now at a slightly more acute angle. But you can't turn a tanker around just like that!

Almost at the same time it muzzle fire flashed on fore- and afterdeck of the Englishman. Müller pushed the handles up. "Retract! LI, take us down to 30 meters!"

He waited until the chief engineer had given the necessary orders, then he stroke over his beard. "That crazy bastard must have discovered the periscope! No wonder, the sea is calm as a duck pond."

"What now? Do you want to launch the second torpedo at him?"

The cox'n cleared his throat. "15 ... ten ..."

"Wait and see!"

The U-boat's bow raised up again into the horizontal. U-15 was 30 meters deep, unreachable for the English. But the English were now also inversely unassailable for the U-boat.

A noise, not like an explosion, but rather like a piece of cloth ripping apart, suddenly sounded through the water.

"A hit!" Rothe stared at the rounded ceiling of the tube, as if he could penetrate the steel with his eyes to see what was going on outside.

Müller blinked. He hadn't expected a hit anymore. The change of course should have carried the tanker out of the torpedo's course after all, unless ...

"IIWO, reduce to seven knots!" He shook his head in disbelief. "He must have sped up. He turned right into the torpedo!"

"Hard to believe the impact pistol didn't fail in that angle." The IWO grinned like the Cheshire cat. "Sometimes you have to be lucky."

"Wait and see!" Müller spun around on his heels, looking to the radio room. "Heidkamp, what is he doing?"

"He's stopping! But I ain't hear any subsequent explosions."

Müller hesitated briefly, then shrugged. "I'll take a look, but just a quick one. Up!"

When the periscope head broke through the surface, the hit tanker appeared almost surreally close due to the optical magnification. "He's really stopping. I think his propellers are running backwards. Can't see any fire though!" He turned again to the stoker who operated the periscope. "Periscope down!"

"Orders, Herr Kaleun?"

"Let's wait and see. Either he lowers his boats because he is sinking, or he makes some provisional repairs and then gets up steam again. In that case we are going to punch him again." Müller leaned against the chart table. "Well, so let's wait again!"

"Either way, he's gonna drive all the sea area wild. Can't be long before destroyers show up."

"Yeah, I expect so." Müller frowned. "Do we have coffee left? And maybe the cookie can produce some sandwiches? This will take some time."

Sub-Lieutenant Rader listened to the conversation of his two superiors from his station behind the helmsmen and blinked surprised. Didn't the IWO just say something about destroyers? And the old man just wanted to sit here and devour sandwiches and coffee? Shouldn't they scram it and fast?

5
Sunflower Oil

Saturday, February 3, 1917, 40 miles northwest of Ireland …

"Nothing!" The commander gestured the stoker to retract the periscope. "Heidkamp, anything in your hydrophone?"

"Nothing but the tanker!" The radio operator listened into his device. "His engines are stopped and I can't hear any more pumps."

"Oh, great!" Müller took off his cap. "We've been waiting for almost two hours now, no destroyer, and that son of a bitch won't go deep six either."

"Or just very slowly?" Lieutenant Rothe's face expressed his helplessness. "This is a bloody tanker! If anything, he should have just blown up!"

"Only if she is carrying gasoline or kerosene or maybe diesel oil."

The commander and the IWO turned to Sub-Lieutenant Rader in surprise. "What do you mean by that?"

"Well, obviously he has no combustible oil loaded."

"What else would a tanker carry?"

Andreas Rader shrugged his shoulders. "I wish I knew! Heavy oil comes to my mind, it's very difficult to ignite. Food oils possibly, but basically anything that is liquid and does not explode immediately when hit by a torpedo."

"How in God's name do you know such things, Herr Leutnant?" Rothe looked at his younger comrade with new respect. "That's hardly in a military handbook, is it?"

"Before the war broke out, I wanted to become a teacher, Herr Oberleutnant." Rader blushed. "After the war, maybe…"

Lieutenant Commander Müller nodded. "Teacher? Well, well! Well, then, make me smart. If the oil doesn't burn, will the tanker sink or not? Oil floats, yes?"

"That depends, Herr Kaleun. The closer to the center you've hit him, the more likely he is doomed to sink. The oil runs out, the buoyancy at the front and aft is maintained, so at some point he simply folds up like a pocket knife. Theoretically." Rader shrugged uncertainly.

"If we surface, the guy starts shooting at us, but we can't let him drift neither, can we?" Müller came to a decision. "IWO, you take command, have the bosun muster the gun crew. We'll sneak to his port side before we show up. If he's out for a fight, at least he can bring only one of his pieces to bear."

"Jawohl, Herr Kaleun!"

Sub-Lieutenant Rader cleared his throat. "Any orders for me?"

"You?" Müller smiled narrow. "You come with me topside! How good is your English?"

"Acceptable, Herr Kaleun."

"All the better!" He nodded satisfied. "Then grab the Morse lamp. Heidkamp shall stay on the radio and find out who our guy is talking to."

It took only minutes for U-15 to emerge dripping about a mile behind the damaged ship.

"Hatch is free!" And already the old man spun the handwheel. The hatch opened, Müller climbed on the tower followed by the lookouts and last but not least Sub-Lieutenant Rader. On the foredeck the galley hatch opened and the nuffer and his men appeared on the narrow deck and manned already in a hurry the first rounds up.

"Call him: This is a German warship, surrender!"

Rader lifted the lamp and began to the letters in Morse code – slow and carefully. The Morse alphabet was part of cadet training, but of course U-boat officers did not have much opportunities to practice.

Through his binoculars Müller saw men running back and forth on the tanker, but no one seemed to make an attempt to man the cannon. Then a signal lamp also flashed in the bridge wing of the other ship: "S/T Taurus, we surrender!"

"At least he's wise." Müller bent over the speaking tube. "IWO, ask Heidkamp if he's transmitting."

"He is, but very weak. Heidkamp thinks his power is out and therefore he uses an emergency device."

The commander nodded. "Thank you!" Thoughtfully he looked at the tanker. A nice modern ship and obviously well equipped. He turned to Rader. "Call him: What is your cargo and how is your situation?"

Again the signal lamp clattered and again it took a moment until the English answered: "Sunflower oil from Halifax to Liverpool. Ship is sinking slowly."

"Ask him if he's got enough lifeboats and if they're equipped."

This time it took a little longer and Rader had to ask again. Then the sub-lieutenant turned to the commander. "He says he has equipped two boats with mast and sails."

"Very nice! He's got ten minutes to get the boats in the water. The Irish coast is about 40 miles in one-seven-zero." The old man grinned mirthlessly. "They'll have a cold night, but they can make it in about ten hours. With the wind stays this way, maybe even a little faster."

Rader tapped the message over to the tanker and the Englishman took the time to confirm it before actually launching the boats. A quarter of an hour later the two full lifeboats sailed away to the distant Irish coast. Müller took a moment to watch their sail handling, then he nodded slightly. "They know what they're doing, no need to worry about that at least." He bent over the tower parapet. "Deck Gun! Fire at will. Kick him under water, buffer!"

The bosun must have waited with the hand on the trigger, because the first shot cracked almost instantly.

"A hit!" Sub-Lieutenant Rader saw with big eyes how the shell detonated in the waterline of the ship.

"Yes, a hit!" Müller smiled at the excitement. "Wouldn't it be a miracle if it wasn't, a mile away and at a non-moving target, right?"

The sub-lieutenant pondered about it for a moment, then he agreed. "Yes, that's true, Herr Kaleun."

The old man lifted the binoculars and looked at the floating ship. "You see? He caught the tin fish pretty far aft."

"A hole as big as a barn door!" The sub-lieutenant looked at the tanker. "Didn't sound so loud underwater, I mean."

"No, it never does." Müller frowned. "So, sunflower oil? What are they doing with the stuff? Butter substitute?"

"Maybe... or nitroglycerin."

"Nitrogly..." Muller, perplexed, lowered the glasses. "Explosives? Then we'd better keep more distance?"

"Don't worry, sunflower oil won't explode. But it can be used to produce explosives. It's also done in Germany; we don't have any palm or coconut oil left."

The old man let the air hiss out of his lungs. "Well, from your lips to God's ears! And that's what you want to teach the kids at school? Chemistry?"

"I hope to study and teach mathematics after the war."

"Mathematics... well, that explains a lot!"

The third and fourth shell struck the floating ship and the list increased more and more. But it cost the bosun almost 20 hits before the tanker finally rolled over and sank. Rader was right. Sunflower oil didn't explode, the stuff didn't even burn.

An hour later, again on a westerly course, the lookout guards spotted a thin plume of smoke on the horizon and U-15 dove away. At a depth of 25 meters Heidkamp could hear the whistling of turbines in the hydrophone. That was a destroyer, if not a cruiser. Too fast to attack from underwater, and too heavily armed to take him on on the surface. But one warship alone could hardly hunt a U-boat. Slow and silently, U-15 snuck away.

6
Bets

Sunday, 4 February 1917, 45 miles north of Ireland ...

Boatswain`s Mate Kern looked at Willemann with a shrug. "What do you say now?"

"About what?"

"About Rader?" Kern grinned. "I was on duty on the tower when we iced the tanker. Looks like the sub-lieutenant's a smart guy. Even the old man was impressed."

"Pah, the IIWO!" Hinze, who had listened to the conversation, rejected Kern's evaluation of Rader. "It's just one more officer. They're all so drunk on their own importance that they can barely see out of their eyes." He distorted his voice a little. "Die a hero's death for Emperor and Fatherland!"

Kern frowned automatically. Hinze sounded almost like Willemann. That wasn't good, that wasn't good at all. Especially not out here, far from home port. But while he was still thinking about what to say about it, Heidkamp, the radio operator and paramedic, was already stretching his head out of the upper bunk. "You're talking shit, and you know it, Hinze!"

"You are hanging around in your radio room all the time, where things are comfortable and it's nice and close to the tower. You should go engine watches for a change." Hinze lowered his voice. "When you're aft, all the way aft in our tube, it's like you're cut off from the world. If the boat goes to the bottom, you won't know till you're already drowning. And from back there there is no way, you make it to the hatch. Heroic death, pah! If we get busted, we'll drown like rats. Rat death, so to speak."

"If you ain't understand no fun, then you shouldn't join the submariners." Heidkamp grinned. "You've already been to the fleet before, right? Got cold feet after the Doggerbank?"

"You weren't there, you can have a big mouth now! After the Limeys pounded Blücher to hell, we ran as fast as we could, while our poor comrades on that armored cruiser drowned for the fatherland. And then I also served on Seydlitz in the summer of '16. You can bet I remember Jutland, when the heavy calibers howled through the air, when Pommern blew up in flames after a torpedo hit, when Lützow got a beating and Frauenlob and Elbing and Wiesbaden sank with all hands. Where have you been?"

"On a U-boat!" Kern leaned back. "We did more to win the war than you did with your capital ships, didn't we?"

"Win the war? You can go whistle for it anyway the way it looks now."

"Man, shut the fuck up!"

"Why?" Hinze stared angrily at Heidkamp. "Are gonna tell me in at the officers?"

"No, of course not." Heidkamp answered Hinze's stare with a calm glance. "Just shut the fuck up!"

For a moment, the electrician peered at the radio operator furiously, but then he backed off. "Pah, you just don't have a clue. We beat the Limeys back then, but the price was high, so damn high, and it didn't bring us anything. They're still blockading us."

Silence fell over the bow compartment. There it was again, that word. Blockade! England had cut off Germany from trade over sea since the beginning of the war. The Limeys were allowed to stop war-important shipments according to all international laws, but they had also cut off all food supplies. Before the war, many things had come from the colonies. Now there had already been cases of beriberi and scurvy amongst the civilian population ... illnesses which even the sailors before the war had known only from old stories. Civilians! That was one of those words too. For the sailors it meant their families, who looked a little more haggard and fragile every time they came home. Many were angry and this anger was looking for an outlet. The emperor, the politicians, the officers, it did not matter, the anger simply needed a target. Heidkamp did understand Hinze. Just like the stoker, he had a wife and children at home – and if he was honest, he wanted nothing more than exactly what Hinze wanted: that this whole damn war would soon be over. Only until then things had to move on by hook or by crook. It was that simple. You couldn't just give up. If Germany lost the war, the other great powers would fricassee the Germans. They could write off the colonies anyway and after this mess the victors would grab anything that wasn't nailed down. How was the homeland supposed to recover from that? Germany simply could not afford to lose the war. And besides, a flag oath was a flag oath. You couldn't just run away from that when things went bad. But yes, Heidkamp understood the stoker. Outwardly calm, he leaned back and looked at Kern. "And what did you think of Rader?"

The Boatswain`s Mate blinked. "There may be more to this boy than meets the eye. Maybe not a good officer, I dunno, but he's bright after all!"

*

Of course the sunken tanker was the subject of conversation in the officers' mess, and also, as it was an officers' mess, everyone held back a little with his opinion. Lieutenant Rothe was on watch, thus chief engineer Wilhelm Klempke and Andreas Rader, the IIWO, were alone for the moment. But a submarine was built like a railroad car after all. There was always someone coming through on the way from front to aft or vice versa. On a submarine, there was no privacy, no room for truly confidential conversations. Even the commander's chamber was only separated from the rest of the milling life by a curtain.

The officers literally lived between the men they had to lead, in a technical world that could fail anywhere at any moment, in a war where one never knew who was hunter and who was hunted, and where the prospects of winning became bleaker by the month. They could rarely express their own worries and thoughts freely, for any insecurity would spread in the boat like the flu, and insecurity at the wrong moment could destroy a boat's crew as quickly as an enemy's shell. All too often officers were not drunk on their own importance, but petrified by the fear of committing a fatal mistake, and thus, even the most important factor, the one determining their whole existence was hardly a suitable subject for a conversation in the wardroom of a submarine. The LI and IIWO were therefore limited to the events of the previous day – strictly apolitical, of course.

"So sunflower oil?"

Rader nodded. "Everything is scarce in war. Armies have to be supplied, but all the men are at war, so they produce nothing. Even for the Limeys it is difficult, although they can import their raw materials from all over the world. So they fall back on whatever's easier to get."

"Sunflower oil is used to replace butter, right?"

The young sub-lieutenant nodded. "Margarine, frying fat, but of course it's also used as a raw material to manufacture all sorts of things. Explosives, antifreeze. I've read that some chemists would think it could even be used to make lube oil or petroleum substitutes."

The chief engineer blinked. "Then we can run our boat on sunflower oil?"

"Of course, it would have to be chemically processed." Rader seriously thought about it. "Of course I'm not a chemist, I have no idea how this works in detail, but a tanker full of that stuff could probably run an entire U-boat squadron for a month."

"Good thing it's on the bottom of the sea then. It sure hurts the English."

Rader looked at the LI with a mixture of amusement and horror. "You think that was the only one?"

"Of course not." The chief engineer looked around baffled. "But every little bit helps."

Andreas Rader also blinked and looked over his shoulder, but none of the men seemed to be nearby. Slowly he nodded. "Yeah, that's one way to look at it."

"You know, Herr Rader? I think that's the only way you can see it." The LI leaned back a little more comfortably on the lower berth. "We still have five torpedoes. Four in the tubes and one in reserve. When we deliver these, we can go home. Maybe not a long vacation, but a little shore leave can brighten up the mood of the men again."

"Yes, of course, but..."

"Nothing but, Herr Leutnant!" Klempke interrupted the IIWO. "We all hope and pray that you're right about your suspicion of a convoy! Then we can push some limeys below deck and set a course back home. And that's all Jack Tar and Johnny Sailor cares about, isn't it?"

"I'm just wondering why we got a single vessel when the English really do put it all together in convoys." Sub-Lieutenant Rader rubbed his thin beard growth. "Of course, something can always go awry with such a large organization ..."

"Oh, damn it! Pray the tanker was just a mistake by some paper warrior. Pray that this godforsaken convoy is on its way and that we can sink a few ships out of it. Because if we don't, we'll hang out here until we run out of gas, and this may take a while hanging out here like the harbor hookers."

"But when our torpedoes are fired, we have to go home." Rader smiled shyly. "Yes, I understand."

"Very good!" Lieutenant Klempke got on his toes. "I'm going aft to check on the front starboard engine. It produced a noise yesterday that I didn't like at all." He bent over to the other bunk. "What are you reading?"

Rader raised the book so the LI could read the title. The sub-lieutenant pulled a disgusted face. "Norman Angell? And then in English?"

"Well, interesting stuff, especially from a mathematical perspective."

"And what does Herr Angell have to say?"

"To put it simple, war is a disaster for the economy."

Klempke smirked sourly. "Well, I could have told you that without reading a book."

The sub-lieutenant looked after LI Klempke, who disappeared aft. Of course, the war was a disaster on all fronts, including the economy. Rader was a thinker. He knew what was being spoken. Most of his time aboard, he spent silently listening. Of course, the men had views. In the crew there were monarchists, democrats, a few communists and of course, as always, the silent majority. Everybody had ideas about what would or should come after the war. Obviously not only in Germany. The problem for Rader was that his world consisted of mathematics, of clean, clear equations and none of these ideas held any water, in a mathematical view. It made no sense, but what made sense anyway in a war like this?

7
The Enemy

Tuesday, 6 February 1917, 38 miles north of Ireland ...

"What do you have?"

The radio operator briefly looked up to Lieutenant Commander Müller. "Destroyers, one or two so far! They're racing back and forth like scalded cats. At least 20 knots, but they are still far away."

"What's their bearing now?"

Heidkamp turned the handwheel. "The first one is aboutish in zero-seven-five, moving to the right fast. The other one is making a turn in zero-eight-eight right now."

The bearings assembled in Müller's head automatically into a picture. Both warships were on starboard, and since U-15 was moving submerged towards the coast, starboard was currently in the west. So those destroyers came either out of the Atlantic or from the high north, from Scapa, and were now heading for the Irish Sea.

"How far are they, what do you think?"

"Far. At least 20 miles, maybe even 30 considering all the ruckus they make."

Müller nodded. "They're searching the convoy route." He came to a decision. "We're gonna stay underwater for a while, I guess there are more still coming. Keep an ear on them."

"Yes, Herr Kaleun!"

"Very good, I'll be at the officer's mess. Have someone fetch me if anything changes."

When Müller entered the mess, all eyes turned at him, but he quickly waved off. "Enjoy your breakfast, gentlemen." He grinned. "Nothing's going to happen for the next few hours. We'll stay submerged."

Max Rothe frowned. "Trouble incoming?"

"The Limeys are once again searching the convoy lanes for submarines." Müller appeared unimpressed. "They zigzag back and forth like crazy. At this speed, they may cross right over our boat now without even noticing we are here. We'll stay under water and sneak a little out of their way, then we should be fine."

"You'd think they'd learned by now this doesn't work." Lieutenant Klempke shook his head.

"It always takes years for all the old heads in higher positions to be replaced. Until then, you will still find officers in commands who still think in the categories of the Crimean War." Müller reached for the bread. "And before all have learned their trade, peace will break out again."

"Oh, great! And in 20, 30 or 40 years our children and grandchildren will start the whole mess all over again?"

"It was always like that, wasn't it, Herr Rothe?" Müller looked at the IWO probing. "Grandchildren? You don't even have children yet. Or did I miss something?"

Rothe blushes a little. "We're expecting our first. The doctors say in summer."

"Well then, my congratulations, Herr Oberleutnant!"

"Now all I have to do is survive the damn war, don't I?"

Müller chuckled. "Well, let's see what we can do." He looked around. "Rader's on watch?"

"Shall I call him?"

"No, it's alright." The commander took some of the honey substitute. "Just when he's back, someone should tell him what those English destroyers mean."

"That they're trying to clear a convoy's route of submarines?"

"Yes. Looks like he was right."

"If they're trying to drive us away now, the convoy must be close." Rothe frowned again. "They put a lot of work in it, don't they?"

"Who, the Englishmen?"

"Yes, I mean..."

"I know what you mean, Herr Rothe." Müller shook his head. "We have declared unrestricted submarine warfare. For the second time. Of course, they have their ideas about where we lie in wait for their cargo ships. Especially now that we've knocked over that tanker."

"So now we wonder thereto they evade to avoid us?"

Müller smirked a little crooked. "Right, and the Limeys then wonder again to which conclusions we came and try not to sail through where we're lurking for them after thinking about the whole problem."

In Rothe's face a big question mark appeared. "How?"

"We're staying here!" The old man smiled again. "Because the English obviously thought, we think, they're trying another route, closer to Scotland. So they come through here because they think we're gone north in the meantime."

The IWO looked at the commander doubtfully. "Unless the Limeys don't think as much as we do, isn't it?"

*

Hours later smoke columns over the horizon were the only thing to be seen of the British warships. U-15 had surfaced already. The tower watch gazed back at the fume pillars almost relaxed. In the gray sea, the U-boat was practically invisible over a distance of two miles and the Limeys never did come even that near to this distance.

Sub-Lieutenant Rader watched the commander from the side. Outwardly calm and serene, the old man leaned on the tower parapet, looked after the Englishmen and smoked a cigar. "Looks like the Limeys didn't learn as much as I thought they did."

"War is madness, held together by chance. Someone overlooks something and... well, then suddenly everything is completely different again."

"Ziethen, Herr Leutnant?"

Rader shrugged. "It seems appropriate, doesn't it?"

"Ziethen was a hussar!" Müller produced a few billows of smoke. "How he would fit to submarine warfare is what I fail to see."

"It is the mathematics of war, Herr Kaleun."

"And I thought that one was von Clausewitz?" Müller peeked at Rader curiously. "So, what has your war mathematics to say about our situation?"

Andreas Rader quickly looked at the lookouts of his watch. "Hey, don't loiter like limp dishrags!" He forced himself into a big grin. "They're gone, the convoy's coming from there!" He pointed aft. "Eyes to your sectors, boys!" He turned to the commander again. "I should be glad I was right, but somehow…" The young sub-lieutenant hesitated.

Müller looked at the cigar in his hand thoughtfully. "You're right. It means the Limeys knew at least three weeks before us that we would resume the unrestricted submarine warfare. They must have some pretty shrewd spies somewhere."

"If that's right, they've been spying for a long time." Sub-Lieutenant Rader watched the smoke billows from the skipper's cigar fainting in the air. "The High Sea's Fleet is neutralized in Wilhelmshaven because the capital ships can't get out without the English knowing in time to intercept them. If they have spies who send a radio message to England, every time one of the battle wagons moves, somebody from our side must have conceived this idea before."

"And that means in your mathematics of war?"

Rader was thinking. "That means someone who understands more about it has to have been looking for these spies for at least two years, but so far they haven't found one. But – as things appear – there must be so many spies, in so many different places, and they can't all be so incredibly good."

"Well?" Müller looked at the sub-lieutenant with renewed interest. "Those Englishmen there…" He pointed at the fading smoke plumes."…had no idea we were hanging out right here. So that's not what their spies told them."

"I don't think the English are the only ones who overlook things from time to time."

"Well, that makes my day … not!" The old man made a sour face. "Anyway, right now it's our turn. The English are obviously planning to slip through here with a convoy. Right here!"

Andreas Rader looked out at the ocean. As far as he could see, the gray watery waste stretched in all directions. Of course, the Ireland's green coast was less than 40 miles away, but from here it was completely out of sight. When one saw the sea this way, it was hard to imagine that barely four sailing hours away people lived peacefully in their homes. But then he admitted to himself that even that was just an illusion. Ireland had its problems too. He felt a bitter taste in his mouth. For thousands of years, people swore that peace and freedom were the highest of all goods, but the only thing people were really good at was killing other people and depriving them of their freedom. Reluctantly he pulled out his pocket watch and studied the dial. Only two hours till sunset. He looked out again at the gray sea. Tonight they would attack a convoy and more people would die at a point in this watery desert that differed in nothing from an endless number of other points in the very same watery desert. Tonight the English would die, tomorrow the turn maybe came to them. War itself was indifferent to nationalities. Rader took a deep breath. "Tonight! Right here!"

Müller nodded and looked at his IIWO with almost cynical amusement. "And what does the mathematics of war say about the fact that we have only five torpedoes left? We can hardly do too much damage with that arsenal, can we?"

The sub-lieutenant tried to give his voice a firm sound. "You know what they say: "Every little bit helps!"

"When you look at it that way…"

8
The Convoy

Wednesday, 7 February 1917, 38 miles north of Ireland ... shortly after midnight

"What do you hear, Heidkamp?"

The radio operator slowly turned the hand wheel of the hydrophone. "At least four, one of them sounds higher pitched."

"Destroyer?"

"Could be." Heidkamp listened strained. "Funny, it's only one."

"There're more of them, they're just not in range yet." Commander Müller slapped the radio operator on the shoulder. "Well done, Heidkamp."

When he returned to the control room, all eyes were on him. He forced a satisfied grin on his face. "Sub-Lieutenant Rader, the radio operator hears your convoy. Four ships so far, one of them probably a destroyer."

"That was to be expected." The sub-lieutenant looked at the skipper uncertainly. "Convoys only make sense if the Limeys protect them too, Herr Kaleun!"

"Won't do them much good this time." Müller looked around. "Moon times, please? It's already risen."

"It should disappear just after 1 o'clock, Herr Kaleun!"

"Already in an hour?" Müller looked disappointed. "We couldn't even reach them when emerged within an hour!"

Rothe, the IWO, seemed not bothered at all. "With all due respect, Herr Kaleun, but they're coming to us anyway," he replied.

"Right again." The commander thought for a moment. "All right, we'll emerge, air the boat, then we'll wait for the British gentlemen to slowly saunter our way before we disappear in the basement again."

"Underwater attack with the bow tubes?"

"Yeah, looks like it. If the Brits let us, we'll turn the boat around and launch the two tin fishes from the stern tubes as well."

"One destroyer, Herr Kaleun! She can hardly stop us!"

"Wait and see, Rothe, wait and see."

*

Punctually one hour later the fountains along the saddle tanks bubbled up. U-15 was preparing to disappear under water again. "Seven meters, what does Heidkamp have for me?"

The LI spilled out a flood of commands: "Forward down five, aft down two. Blow out cells one and two!"

Slowly, almost sluggishly, the bow sank downwards. The con mate sang out the changing depths, "Three meters, four meters, four meters..."

"Boat doesn't follow!"

"Blow out control tank!" The voice of the chief engineer sounded sharp.

The air hissed out of another tank. The LI counted the seconds. "Blow out cells five and six!"

"Six meters!"

"And dive planes zero!"

"Seven meters!" And a moment later again: "Seven meters!"

The chief engineer raised his hand to his dirty cap. "Boat is at seven meters, Herr Kaleun."

"A little bitchy today, the lady?"

"Well, the trim changes every day." The LI shrugged it off. "We consume food and fresh water. The boat gets lighter every day."

"It's all right. But keep an eye on it, Herr Klempke." Müller blinked. "Not that diving takes that long when a limey destroyer is chewing on our asses."

"Jawohl, Herr Kaleun!"

"All right, Herr Rothe: You take the con, I'm in the radio booth."

Sub-Lieutenant Rader had observed the diving maneuver with growing restlessness. Sometimes a submarine would dive a little slow. As the chief engineer had told the commander, the crew consumed provisions and fresh water. A submarine at sea was getting lighter all the time. In a few days 36 men ate a few hundred kilos of weight in food and that was reflected in the trim balance as a few hundred kilos more buoyancy. One should think that's not much compared to the weight of the whole U-boat, but from a technical point of view a submarine balanced always just at the border between swimming and sinking. The difference between surface sailing and underwater march was about two tons of water in the diving cells, and compared to just two tons a few hundred kilos made the difference between fast diving, slow diving or – if things came worse – no diving at all. Once the boat was under water, they could dynamically change the depth with the dive planes, but first those things had to be under water to work.

Rader felt his stomach cramp a little. Had LI Klempke just dropped the ball or was there another reason why the boat was diving so hesitantly? He did not dare to imagine how things might have played out if the old man would have followed his original plan and attacked the English on the surface. What if they would have to dive away quickly from a pissed destroyer and then the boat would play bitchy… he watched Rothe giving some orders to the helmsmen. Calm and controlled. Sometimes he wished he would be like the IWO. But perhaps the lieutenant was only so nonchalant because he lacked the imagination to picture the imminent catastrophe. Andreas Rader had that imagination, and many times, when he had been laying on his bunk at night, he had seen the green, glassy wall of water break through the torn hull of this damn iron tube drowning them all. Submariners did not die in dignity for Emperor and Fatherland – submariners drowned like rats in a trap. Then again, who did really die dignified in war?

*

Otto Heidkamp carefully turned the hand wheel once more by a few degrees. "Ain't easy to say, the water is still stirred up by the diving maneuver."

"Take your time, Heidkamp." Müller leaned in the bulkhead frame. "They must still be a few miles away."

"Jawohl, Herr Kaleun."

Müller turned around. His glance met a young sailor who had pressed himself against the wall of the radio room. The man was supposed to be in the bow compartment right now, but that very room was so damn far away from the tower hatch. There was always someone who tried to sneak closer to the control room. Maybe he wasn't even aware of it, but in a submerged submarine stress and fear reigned, especially over the younger ones. The commander smiled briefly as the young man looked at him with widened eyes. "Müller! Stand here, right next to the bulkhead frame."

"Herr Kaleun?"

"And here you stay and pass everything the radio operator has to report on to control room!"

"Jawohl, Herr Kaleun!"

The two unequal Müllers spun around when they heard the radio operator. "Gotcha! Straight bearing zero! Cargo vessel!" With closed eyes Heidkamp turned the wheel carefully back and forth. "Destroyer, three degrees starboard."

"Distance?"

"I'm not sure, three miles, maybe more. She's running pretty fast!"

Commander Müller looked for a second surprised. "But not directly at us, I hope?"

"Nah ... I think, she's cruising in front of that big-ass freighter!" The radio operator closed his eyes again. "There's more behind her. A whole bunch, Herr Kaleun."

The old man nodded sharply. "Well, then, let's see if we can smash some of them to smithereens!"

*

"2,000 meters!"

"What did you say?" E-mate Hinze looked through the open bulkhead from the E-machine room.

"2,000 meters the sea is deep here." The diesel stoker Willemann shrugged his shoulders. It was quiet here astern. Only the electric engines were humming on low revs.

"It's dark and cold. If the Limeys send us down there, we'll have peace!"

"You old croaker!" Hinze shook his head. "The old man knows what he's doing. That one, the Brits will hardly haul over the coals that easy!"

"Pah, the old man! Officer of the new school. They're all only out for a Blue Max!"

"Yeah, yeah, I know." Hinze forced himself to shrug. Of course Willemann was afraid. They were as far astern from the con as one could get on a submarine. The only connection forward were the speaking tubes. The old man never ordered the bulkheads to close before an attack. The boat consisted of three sections, but if only one was flooded, it went anyway straight down to the bottom. In the Baltic there might still be a chance to escape from a department if the boat went down, but not here. 2,000 meters, Willemann had said.

But the hatch to the engine room was a different matter. Should something go wrong, perhaps a short circuit, a petroleum fire or whatever more of possible technical disasters could happen, then the bulkhead had to be closed to prevent the whole boat from being filled with smoke. The engine bulkhead was always closed and so the two engine rooms for the petroleum engines and the electric engines of a submarine became the loneliest spots imaginable. Cut off from all knowledge of what was going on, the men sat around waiting for an order to start their gasoline motors or for the electric engine stokers to change the speed. But most of the time, they just waited. For orders or that the boat was attacked by a destroyer. For a word from the con telling them that they got away once again, or the dull rumbling of water bombs in the depths, indicating to them that the Limeys were after them.

*

For a moment he could only see blackness, then the periscope broke through the surface. At first he saw a few splashes of water, then something less dark in the night, but before he really understood, the wave rolled over the periscope head. "Get the asparagus higher out!"

Behind him he heard a few commands as the LI brought the boat a little closer to the surface. It was a maneuver calling for knowledge and finesse, but Klempke knew what he was doing. Almost in slow motion the commander's field of vision shifted higher over the dark sea ... and then, suddenly, he spotted the English. Not more than darker shadows in the dark night. The moon hung already low in the sky and its silver gleam shone only weakly on the perpetually moving sea. But amidst the darkness between the faint reflections was something that did not change. Ships! Müller held his breath. Those were more than he had expected!

"How many has Heidkamp now?"

"At least half a dozen freighters and three destroyers!"

Three! Three were a lot against one submarine! Müller looked through the periscope again and this time he could see a slightly brighter silhouette. That had to be one of them, but he couldn't make out any details. Three were too much for one sub when they had time and space ... only these three were hampered by a whole convoy and the darkness. They could not navigate freely and the noise caused by the cargo ships disturbed their hydrophone. He let go of the asparagus' handles and nodded to the stoker. "Periscope down!"

For a moment he pondered, then he saw the expectant faces and grinned. "That must be more than six. Heidkamp probably hears only the leading ships."

"And probably not all the destroyers either?"

Müller nodded and looked at the IWO calmly. "No, probably not. There will be always one drifting and listening."

"So at least four?" Rothe made a slightly worried face.

"I suppose so!"

"And you want to take the convoy from the flank, then cross through to the other side to fire the stern tubes?"

Müller raised his eyebrows. "Leutnant Rader, now please tell me you calculated this and I'm not that predictable!"

Andreas Rader contorted his face. "It appears logical. It will also seem logical to the Brits when the first torpedoes find their targets."

To everyone's surprise, the commander grinned again. "I'm glad we agree, Herr Leutnant." For a moment he enjoyed the astonished expressions on their faces, then he nodded. "We take the convoy from starboard, launch the bow torpedoes, dive under the convoy, and when the Limeys are sure we want to go to the other side, we start silent running and double back."

Max Rothe blinked. "This can work, Herr Kaleun!"

"No!" Müller pushed the cap a little bolder to the side. "This will work."

9
Torpedoes away!

Wednesday, 7 February 1917, 38 miles north of Ireland … shortly after midnight

"Two… three… four…"

The IWO jotted down the numbers from the periscope's rotating ring. Just don't screw up now! Five seconds, if the old man had estimated the distance correctly, it was the speed of the target. If not, or if he had misread the angles, or if the ship suddenly zagged, then the precious tin fishes would be wasted. There were a dozen things that could go awry with a torpedo shot – at least a dozen.

Müller ignored the IWO. Rothe knew his business. He waited until the sailor who sang out the seconds on the stopwatch reached the "six", then he swung the periscope around again. For a moment water splashes covered again his view at the sea, then a slightly brighter silhouette emerged from the night. High bow wave! That escort was fast, but that was the way the destroyers hunted for submarines: A sprint with high speed, then they stopped their engines, drifted and listened. Not only would they hear better; for their engines were not running, they would also be hidden from the hydrophone of a submarine, because the U-boat could only hear whatever was producing noises. Sprint and drift was the tactics of the British destroyers, and when they discovered an U-boat while listening, they threw depth charges and tried to drive the iron shark to the surface, where they finished him with their guns, or, should it happen, simply rammed the sub to send it down forever with all hands aboard.

The old man watched the destroyer for a moment. As fast as he was already, he would soon start to drift. A smile flew over Müller's face. The limey would drift in the wrong direction. Müller saw the slender stern swing further around and the four stacks almost forming a line in his periscope. It was only a slight reddish shimmer, fire from the hell of its boilers that made the warship visible at all, but in a dark night that was enough to give a ship away. Müller turned the optic in circles, but he could not make out any of the other two escorts. This could mean that they continued to pay attention to the convoy, that one was running on the other side of the convoy, or that one or both were floating and listening somewhere in the dark, ready to suddenly start and make the invisible hunter the hunted.

"IWO, when you're ready?"

"New course will be 70 degrees, Herr Kaleun."

"Very well! Then take her around then, Herr Rothe."

"Yes, Herr Kaleun!"

Müller focused again on the periscope. Normally, in daylight, he wouldn't have risked leaving the asparagus up for this long, but at night the Limeys had little chance of discovering the periscope, even if, as now, it protruded quite far out of the water because of the swell. If he already had problems spotting a full-size merchantman, then it had to be much harder for the Limeys!

Müller sensed the boat laying slightly over to the side and in his optics, the sea surface seemed to tilt. Not much, maybe two or three degrees, but it still was a little distracting. He swiveled the handles around to keep an eye on the target. 70 degrees… after the IWO had finished the course change, the bow of the boat would point to an invisible point in the water, the first freighter would also pass if she remained on her current course. Basically Müller had to aim the whole boat at that point and fire the tin fish at the right moment. The whole trick was that both arrived at this point at the same time. But that also meant that for long minutes, he could not change course or depth. Should a destroyer start his engines now …

He turned the periscope further to port. There was the one destroyer he had seen before, still on a course out from them. Where the hell were the others?

"What's up, Heidkamp?"

It took a moment and in the meantime he heard the IWO commanding again: "Helm aloft, steer zero-seven-zero!"

"Yes, Herr Leutnant!"

"From radio shack, Herr Kaleun! At least a dozen freighters, turbine in two-six-five, turbine in three-four-five!"

Two! One was the destroyer running off on port, the other one stood almost dead ahead, somewhere behind the freighter, and the third had to drift and listen somewhere else. Müller suppressed the impulse to cuss out loud. Instead, he just shrugged it off. "Alright then! Flood all tubes, open outer torpedo doors!"

He turned the periscope back into the bearing of the first freighter. A small bow wave, just a few splashes and a massive shadow behind it. Müller held his breath. That guy was big – bigger than he had thought at first. "IWO, we launch tube I and II at the first merchantman. He's a pretty fat one. Tube III on the one behind him."

"Jawohl, Herr Kaleun! 30 seconds!"

Müller checked the bearing again. "He's coming up slowly."

"20 seconds!"

The old man banished everything else from his mind and kept the periscope pointed at the target. The IWO would now keep a zealous watch over the bearing ring. Silence hung over the control room.

"Ten!"

Müller raised his hand. "Ready to fire!"

"Five!"

"Tube I… gooo! Tube II… gooo!"

The boat shook under his feet, from the bow he heard air escape from a valve as the LI flooded one of the trim cells.

"Torpedoes running!"

He waited a moment, no longer than a few heartbeats, then turned the asparagus at the second freighter. Much smaller. He took a deep breath. Wait… wait… the third shot was more or less a matter of luck. "IWO, zero-six-zero!"

"Yes, Herr Kaleun, zero-six-zero!"

Again the sea tilted in its optics, this time to the other side. Wait … even when the sea was horizontal again, he waited a moment. Let the boat rest on the new course. The change of course had reduced the distance the torpedo had to run. "Tube III… gooo!"

He heard the order being passed through the speaking tubes, but the hissing of the compressed air and the slight shaking of the boat were confirmation enough. The third tin fish was on its way.

"Close the bow doors!"

He turned the periscope in a semicircle. There was the first destroyer ... then the second appeared out of the darkness, a gray silhouette with a higher bow wave. But still far away. Far... what was far in a night like this? He was maybe 1,400 meters away, maybe only 1,000? With high speed the escort ship could stand over them in a minute and cover them with depth charges if he figured now, what was happening.

"Herr Kaleun! Destroyer running up his engines in zero-four-five!"

Müller spun the periscope into the bearing, that had been called out from the radio shack. There he was, the third destroyer! He must have really been adrift listening! The pieces of the puzzle came together. The gentleman hadn't heard the low electric machines, but now he had noticed the torpedoes.

Müller saw the warship swinging around in a tight circle like a door. Along the bow and almost a third of his length, water splashed as his engines spun up to maximum revs and he simultaneously laid the rudder hard over. Müller drew a grimace. Despite the impressive sight, he would still need to long to pick up speed again.

The destroyer commander must have come to the same conclusion, because on the bridge of the warship a signal light flashed up in hectic staccato. Müller let go of the handles and took a step back. "Retract periscope!"

He turned around. "New course will be zero-one-zero! LI, bring us down to 30 meters!"

His number one tipped at his cap and wanted to confirm but there a series of noises hit the boat. At first they heard the impact of a torpedo, this unmistakable sound that sounded rather like tearing apart a piece of cloth than a real explosion, but then, as they waited for the second impact, suddenly a dull rumble rolled through the water.

Instinctively, everyone grabbed for hold. "Depth charges?"

The commander blinked and looked at the IWO who had asked the question. Probingly, he let go of the pipe he had been holding on to. The boat didn't shake, rear up or anything else untoward, it just followed calmly its course. "LI, 30 meters, now! IWO, get us on the new heading!"

Sub-Lieutenant Rader stood at the chart table next to the coxswain and closed his eyes for a moment. The old man looked at him thoughtfully from behind while the IWO and LI went through the litany of changing course and depth. When the young sub-lieutenant opened his eyes again, he nodded to him briefly. "Must have loaded some ammo."

Rader cleared his throat. "Probably!" He turned to the cheering men at control room. "Now cool it again here, work is not finished yet!"

The old man turned around again. Rader understood. Those weren't water bombs, that was a different kind of explosion. The big cargo ship must have been erupted when the loaded ammunition blew up. A big ship, about 40 men crew or more, and now it was gone, as if the bucket and the men on him never existed.

The bow of the submarine decreased slightly and he heard the con mate sing out the depth. "Nine… ten… ten… eleven…"

"Faster, LI! Flood the control tank too!"

"Jawohl, flooding control tank!"

Müller looked over his shoulder to the bulkhead. "Heidkamp! What's the destroyer doing?"

"Heads zero-seven-zero, still picking up speed!"

Zero-seven-zero! The man o' war had no contact, he headed for the position from where they had fired the torpedoes. No wonder he didn't hear it when he tried to get going with all his might. His own machines interfered with his hydrophone!

Müller relaxed a little. Even when some depth charges blasted in some distance, he didn't move. Far! The Limeys had no contact.

"20 … 21 …"

"Pull her out, LI!"

Klempke nodded. "Dive planes zero!"

Slowly the bow came up. Müller granted himself a sigh. "If the convoy doesn't zag out of its heading, we'll be right under the cargo ships in five minutes." He raised apparently untouched his hands and grinned. "We sunk an ammunition freighter, with the third tin fish, I probably shot Maggie's drawers!"

The IWO looked at him and answered his grin. "Happens in the best families, Herr Kaleun, but we got the big boy, he's on the account. How big do you think he was?"

The old man frowned. "Six, six and a half thousand tons. Big anyway!" He snapped his fingers. "Heidkamp, what are the Englishmen doing?"

"The destroyer seems to be turning, now he's bearing in zero-nine-zero! The other one runs rather half ahead in two-two-five. I don't hear the third one! Another Freighter is coming up from two-eight-zero."

The lieutenant commander hinted a nod. "Very well, thank you, Heidkamp." In his head, the bearings united into a picture. The convoy was stubbornly keeping its original heading. In a few minutes they would be under the first freighters and the English destroyers could not attack them there. Apart from the fact that the heavy engines of the steamers would simply drown out any noise of their low electric engines anyway. For minutes, it would be for the hunting destroyers as if the German U-boat would just have disappeared. At least, till Müller turned around to fire his stern tubes. The last two tin fishes! If he could bring those in a target, it would be a successful patrol and they could back out of here and set course home!

Müller had to force himself to regain focus. "Heidkamp, keep singing out the bearings!" He briefly looked through the bulkhead to the radio shack. The young sailor and his namesake still stood at the hatch. "Müller, pass everything on exactly!"

"Yes, Herr Kaleun!"

*

Andreas Rader had squeezed himself in the corner of the aft bulkhead. There wasn't much to do when the boat was submerged. Like most of the men, he waited. Right now, everything in the submarine appeared to work just fine, they were 30 meters under water and headed straight under the freighters. The English destroyers had no contact and the closer they got to the big ships and all the noise they made, the worse their chances became. At the moment it didn't look too bad for U-15. Of course, everything could always change from one moment to the next, that much Rader had already learned about life on submarines, but again, he thought, at the moment it didn't look too bad at all.

With almost physical effort he forced himself to relax. When the attack begun, he had almost jumped from one leg to the other. It didn't cause any difficulties to him to convert the bearings the young sailor announced from next to the radio shack into a coherent picture. One destroyer was still turning, producing so much noise that he would hardly hear anything. The second one seemed to be located far away and was also running high speed. Only the third one, Heidkamp could not detect him and there could only be one reason for that: He drifted with stopped engines on the surface and listened for the sub! That one, they had to pass with enough distance that he would not pick up on them.

"Revolutions for two knots!"

Rader blinked as he heard the old man's voice again. The image in his head changed as the buzzing of the electric engines became a little louder. Two knots, that was about 3.6 kilometers per hour, or in other words: a tiny bit more than one meter per second. The destroyer on starboard would need about a minute to finish his turn and set course for the position from which they had fired their torpedoes. So, plus the minute it had taken him to get back in motion, it all added up to a little over 100 meters that they had since moved away from that spot.

But from the port side approached the convoy. The fat cargo steamers made six knots. So that was another three meters per second! With every second they now covered three times as much distance as the submarine and in about 20 minutes U-15 would be roughly under the center of the convoy. Rader leaned against the cold, wet metal. Nothing went fast with the U-boat weapon, that was for sure. Even the destroyers, the fastest ships he could imagine, ran hardly faster than a large automobile on land. Less than 50 kilometers per hour! 15 meters per second! But that was exactly the problem, wasn't it? Ships were not automobiles, even the smallest ships were still big and heavy things moving through the water. It took time to pick up speed or even just to change course. The salient point was to figure out where one would like to be in ten or twenty minutes. To do that, you had to understand where all the others, the freighters, the destroyers, would be in ten or 20 minutes. A battle at sea was a little bit like playing chess. The trick ... Rader felt an ice-cold shiver running down his back, but before he could say anything, he heard the young sailor at the other bulkhead passing on Heidkamp's reports: "Destroyer starting up, three-three-five! Destroyer's starting up, zero-one-five!" And then, a tiny moment later, "Port destroyer has stopped his engines!"

Rader stared at the commander, unable to say a word. But then Müller pushed his cap back even more daring and smiled. "Well, there he is!" The old man looked around. "I already wondered where he was hiding."

Rader took a deep breath. So the skipper had already expected a fourth destroyer? But why ... the young IIWO felt how the clear image of bearings in his head dissolved into fog. Four destroyers, there was no way in hell, that could work out, wasn't there?

10
The Fog of War

Wednesday, 7 February 1917, 38 miles north of Ireland ... shortly after one o'clock at night

Up on the surface, it had to be dark like in a bear's butt! The moon had already set. Lieutenant Commander Müller tried to imagine the situation with the eyes of the destroyer commanders. Somehow the Limeys had picked up on what little noise their engines produced but the two escorts who now ran up their engines with all they got were headed for the same point: his boat. One of them had to back off or this would become a nice train wreck! But the room they had left was slowly getting tight, the freighters were getting closer and closer, and now all four destroyers were scrambling about on the port side of the convoy. Would the English set lights to avoid collisions or would they risk speeding through the dark out of the fear light would make it easier for him, the sub commander, to shoot another freighter out of their convoy?

Further noises came from the surface, clearly to hear even without the help of a hydrophone. Close, but not too close! Some kind of pitsch pitsch pitsch, too high pitched and too fast for propellers, even for the fast revving destroyer screws, then followed by one ... two ... detonations, strangely flat.

"They're shooting!"

"Thank you, I hear it, IWO." Müller blinked. "They must think we're at periscope depth."

"But it's still damn close!"

"Relax!" The commander looked over his shoulder. "Heidkamp?"

"One coming right at us, still three-three-five, the other one is giving way to starboard!"

So one of the destroyers had cleared the way for the other. When he crept off to starboard, he had actually turned to port, from his point of view! Müller reached for one of the ubiquitous pipelines. "He wants to cover us with depth charges! IWO, change heading on my mark! We turn hard to starboard and shortly after back to port!"

"Yes, Herr Kaleun!"

Minutes passed and appeared to the men like an eternity. With low humming e-machines the boat stubbornly held its course ... and then they heard it. A mechanical rumble over them. At first it was still low, more a hunch, but while they were still listening, it got louder, grew to the loud whistling of turbines. This was not the usual stomping of steam engines; this was a warship and it was obviously running at high speed.

The IWO looked at the old man, but Müller just shook his head. "Wait for it!" And then again, as if he wanted to calm down a nervous horse: "Wait for it!"

A couple of the men just involuntarily ducked a little. It sounded as if the destroyer was almost on top of them, but again the voice of the commander cut through the noise: "Wait!"

Slowly Müller raised his hand. A few more seconds. "Now, rudder starboard hard!"

The helmsman whirled the wheel around. U-15 made only two knots, even with the rudder laying hard starboard the turn felt slow. Almost placid the boat tilted a little to the right. But that was a deception. In fact, the bow swung around like a door. Only inside the tube, it was hard to notice, because every reference point was missing. Only those who looked at the compass could see the rotation. The old man watched the compass needle, while above his U-boat the clatter of the beating propellers almost sounded like a train about to run over him. But it wasn't a train, it was a British destroyer and he wouldn't just rush over him, he'd drop some depth charges on him!

"Rudder hard to port!" In his mind, Müller counted the seconds. "IWO, steer zero-one-zero!"

"Zero..."

The IWO didn't get a chance to finish the confirmation. Out in the sea, the first depth charges exploded. The boat buckled under a hard-double detonation and shook like a battered boxer as the explosions thundered through the depths. For a moment the needle of the depth gauge performed a crazy dance before returning to its original position and pointing to 30.

Then one more explosion, and almost immediately another one. The boat jolted suddenly on the side. Items flew out of lockers, a few light bulbs burst with a loud bang. The propellers above the U-boat boomed as if they were about to knock their heads off. And then a third pair of depth charges detonated.

Men staggered as the boat was buffeted. More glass burst. Somewhere a rivet jumped out of its place and shot like a bullet through the tube. A thin jet of water sprang from the tiny opening and men immediately jumped up to press a few pieces of wood against it. Cross section reduction, the credo of all ship safety technicians, and on a submarine, everyone is something like a professional ship safety technician.

The propellers suddenly beat more on port and the dull rumble of the explosions faded. Pale faces looked at each other, then at the old man. But the commander simply stood in the middle of the control room, his hand on the asparagus, and smiled disparagingly. The men blinked in surprise. Müller looked around. "Now that he did screw up quite nicely, the Limey!" He had to raise his voice a little that the men could hear him, the propellers of the warship above them were still so loud. "Heidkamp! If you hear anything again, find me the other destroyers!" He shook his head in disbelief. "I knew he couldn't follow the turn, but that he'd miss the whole turn..."

Max Rothe had tilted his head a bit and listened to the destroyer sailing off. "What's he doing now?"

Müller shrugged his shoulders. "Not much he can do. Till he's around again and can start another run at us, we're under his convoy. He can hardly push between the freighters with full speed, can he? Such a freighter would just iron over this tin can destroyer."

"How..." But then the IWO nodded. "Yes, I hear it too!"

The men pricked their ears. What were their officers talking about? But then they all heard it too. At first unnoticed, another noise had mixed into the metallic concert on the surface, a muffled, polyphonic pounding. The freighters! The whole convoy couldn't sail far away anymore. Müller grinned. "Herr Rothe, head straight north! «

"Jawohl, Herr Kaleun!"

"LI?"

The engineer appeared behind the valves. "Here!"

"What about the batteries?"

"At this speed? About four hours more!"

"Very nice, enough power then." The old man looked around. "Well, now calm down, men, we're not done yet!"

*

The beating of the cargo ship propellers sounded deeper than that of the destroyers. Most of the buckets used piston engines, but the stomping of them became only audible in the submarine when they were close to a freighter. Most of the time the polyphonic concert of the big propellers drowned out the freighters' engine sounds.

Almost all the men sat or leaned somewhere where they had found a place. For the moment there was silence. The worst damage had already been repaired; the rest had to wait until they could emerge. It was an unreal situation. Up on the surface a few hundred British sailors waited only for their chance to kill them and vice versa they waited for the right time to turn around, return to periscope depth and attack another freighter with the stern tubes. Even if the English assumed that U-15 would dive completely through under the convoy, that the boat would attack at least once more, there could be no doubt for them ... and still nothing happened. Slowly, almost crawling, the boat snuck around under the freighters. Actually, it stood more than it was moving at all. It was the freighters that travelled the actual route and sailed in seemingly endless columns over the submerged U-boat.

Andreas Rader looked at his pocket watch. A quarter past two! Almost half an hour had passed since the destroyer had thrown his depth charges at them. They had passed the outer column of the convoy and were now approaching the second. Despite

Heidkamp's reports he had lost the overview. He couldn't even remember if the convoy had two or three columns. Did anyone ever mention that? Did anybody even know aboard the boat? Or was it just unimportant?

The IIWO tried to imagine the situation on the surface. It had to be totally dark. Had ... should ... of course the Limeys could fire flares or try to search the sea with spotlights, but they wouldn't do it for fear of attracting more submarines. As if Germany had so many submarines at all. Only the English didn't know that – or maybe they did too? Who knew what the other side really knew?

Rader's gaze fell on the commander and the IWO. The two men were standing in the middle of the control room, the IWO leaning relaxed against the periscope shaft, talking quietly as if they didn't even notice that the men around were listening to every word they were saying. As if everything was quite normal, the very normal daily business, as if not a few hundred determined men were waiting topside to kill them. Or at least: as if they didn't mind, because they knew exactly that the English wouldn't get them anyway.

Rader thought again of what von Clausewitz had written about the fog of war. That commanders in war had to make their decisions in the excitement of battle and on the basis of incomplete facts, precisely in the fog of war. The old man didn't know everything, of course not. His picture of the situation was as incomplete as that of his opponents up there on the surface. Which in turn degraded the commander's entire self-confidence to a show. Of course he knew as well as anyone else that he didn't know everything, that such attacks could go wrong, that the English convoy commander might smell the roast, that something in the boat failed, or that one of the destroyers simply got a contact in his hydrophone by luck. Of course, he knew that his picture of the situation was not complete, could not be complete at all. And of course the old man was afraid, maybe even more than anyone else on board. Everyone here feared for his life, it was the instinct of self-preservation that rebelled in everybody in this narrow iron tube. But the commander carried the responsibility for them all on his shoulders. If he screwed up, then they were all finished and nobody could be more aware of that than the old man himself. Nevertheless, he stood there in the middle of the control room and already discussed the trip home with his IWO, as if all of this was just a formality.

But if Rader had difficulties understanding his commander, he had even greater difficulties understanding what the English were doing up there. The convoy stubbornly held its course. Why hadn't the Limeys zagged off? If the freighters changed course, the safe shelter they offered the German boat at the moment from the searching destroyers would be out of reach in a quarter of an hour. So why not? The English still had sufficient space to the north. Why didn't they use it? Did the Limeys know anything they didn't? Something the old man didn't know either?

Dull rumbling rolled once more through the water. Far away. The boat didn't even shake. Nevertheless, the men looked in dazzled.

Commander Müller also blinked in surprise. "What's new?"

"They must think they have a contact." Max Rothe frowned. "They might think they got us, don't they?"

The old man shook his head. "Even they can't be that wrong!"

"Yes, but what are they bombing if not us?"

"That..." Müller blinked again. "That's a really good question!" He turned his head. "Heidkamp?"

"Just the freighters and the depth charges. For a moment there was a destroyer, but I lost him again. Bearing was about three-five-zero, Herr Kaleun!"

Three-five-zero, that was ahead and maybe a mile to port. A mile, that was nothing! In Rader's mind, the bearings automatically assembled into an overview. Confused, he shook his head. "Another submarine?"

"Where should that come from, Herr Rader?" Max Rothe looked at his younger comrade uncertainly.

"From the north." The commander took off his cap and swept over his forehead. "From the north!"

Again explosions rolled through the Irish Sea. Two, four, six... then two more at a short distance.

"Then the comrades gonna get a bad beating."

"Silence in the boat!" The commander put his cap back on. "Depth charges are inaccurate. They'll need luck to hit the other boat. We've experienced it for ourselves. They have to force him to the surface to really hurt him."

Rader suppressed a remark. The other U-boat had tried to sneak up on the northern column and snipe out one or two freighters. That were all the tin fishes of the bow tubes. Only, of course, the other commander had not known that the British destroyers were all waiting on his side for U-15, which was still running north under the convoy. Four destroyers, that was too many if they could concentrate on one target. At some point, one of the charges just had to hit.

"IWO, steer West!" The old man turned around. "Heidkamp, where's the next freighter?"

"Not far, almost 180 degrees."

"Find me the one behind it!" The Commander's eyes found Klempke. "LI, take us to periscope depth."

For a moment, time seemed to stand still and a few men pulled in the air sharply. Then discipline and training regained control. "Periscope depth, jawohl, Herr Kaleun!"

The old man ignored the flood of orders issued by the IWO and LI and turned to Rader: "We are between the columns. So the tubs won't be rushing over our asparagus right away."

The IIWO cleared his throat. "And if we turn around and kill the next freighter in the column, the Limeys know there's two of us and can't concentrate on the other boat alone anymore."

"That's the theory, Herr Rader!" The old man laughed quietly. "Of course, if they're up there as bright as you are, they'll figure out we're the boat that doesn't have any torpedoes left."

"Perhaps not, Herr Kaleun." Andreas Rader paused a second. "We only sank one at the first attack."

"You think they didn't notice the other torpedo?"

"Maybe not?"

The commander stood completely still for a brief moment. "One can hope!" Then he grinned mischievously. "Then better start pray your old man really missed his target on the first try."

"Nine meters... eight..." The voice of the con mate cut into the conversation.

The commander turned away. "Raise periscope!" He pressed his face against the bulge. Then he took a breath. "Bloody sh...!"

"What..."

To everyone's surprise, the commander stepped aside. "Take a look at this for yourself, Herr Rader." He turned around. "Flood the stern tubes, open stern doors!"

The young IIWO pressed his eyes against the rubber bulge. Then he held his breath. It wasn't dark like he expected. Bright light shone on one side of his field of view, but from wherever this light came, the freighters of the second column were still standing between them and the source of the light, sharply outlined as black silhouettes against the glaring shine. The Englishmen could not illuminate the targets more beautifully for them at all!

Behind him he heard the voice of the commander again. "Periscope down!"

Rader stepped back when the asparagus disappeared into the shaft. "Search lights?"

"Too bright for search lights. I assume, they fired flares, they were just already too low when we extended the periscope. They'll be shooting new ones soon!" The old man calculated shortly. "Five minutes, then we'll head south! IIWO, you take care of the course change, IWO ... Max, you take care of the torpedoes. We're launching two single shots, so be prepared!"

The officers saluted and turned to their duties. For a moment the old man stood in the crowded control room, men all around him and yet it was as if he was alone, isolated from everything around. Then he smiled. "And LI... when we get rid of the torpedoes, I want the boat back to depth. 30 meters! Not that we're gonna smash into another one of those freighters."

"Jawohl!"

"Well, let's do it!" He breathed pointedly. "IIWO, new course will be exactly one-eight-zero! IWO, that's also our firing direction! Target speed six, bow right, depth three, that should do it!"

The boat listed a little on its side when pressure came on the rudders and forced the bow into a turn. Müller watched the compass and the numbers running through. The IIWO might have been a bright head, but his mastery of the ship left much to be desired. "Come up, Rader, or you'll overshoot!"

"Port 20." Rader waited a moment. "Counter rudder, steer one-eight-zero!"

Müller saw how the numbers on the compass slowed down. "Very nice!"

Rader suppressed a grin that wanted to sneak up on his face despite the tense situation. He knew quite well, he had still a lot to learn as a sailor. Nevertheless, the old man had let him command the change of course and sent the IWO to do the calculations. Did the man ever forget a detail?

"Raise periscope!"

Rader observed from the corner of his eye how the old man first turned the pipe forwards, then aft. "IWO! Take angles."

Behind them, the con mate began to count the seconds in a monotonous voice: "...three ...four ...five ..."

"Six knots!" Max Rothe looked into his tables. "14, 13 ..."

Instead of changing the heading of the boat and thus the direction of the torpedo, the IWO simply waited until the ship was in the right position to fire the torpedo.

The seconds stretched like rubber, finally Rothe raised his hand. "Tube V, gooo!"

While the boat was still jolting and the LI let flow water into one of the trim cells, he raised his hand again. "Tube VI... go!"

Rader felt the boat buckle again under his feet as the second tin fish left the tube. That's it, now all the tubes were empty. Now they could go home. Anyway, if the destroyers let them. Because if they figured out that they had no torpedoes left, they could also attack ruthlessly, because now the boat was without any defense.

"LI, bring the boat to 30 meters!"

11
One more ...

Wednesday 7 February 1917, 38 miles north of Ireland ... shortly after two o'clock in the morning.

The boat once again tilted a little when the IIWO changed course. At the same time, the bow lowered slightly.

"Nine... ten... eleven..." The con mate counted out the depth again, but Müller noticed the reports only marginally. The motions of his boat told him enough. They went deeper and the boat followed rudder. That was good enough for him right now.

Somewhere outside the tube, they heard a dull rumble over the omnipresent beating of the cargo ship propellers. So the Limeys were still trying to bomb their comrades to pieces. It had to be a German submarine, even if Müller had no clue about its presence before the limeys had started all the ruckus. The range of the radio did not extend as far as the homeland and, conversely, the High Command seldom revealed the location of other boats. Of course the English could listen to the German radio messages and vice versa. The question was, how much could they really read? The transmissions were of course encrypted and everyone assumed that the codes were secure, but who could say such a thing exactly, and if you operated out of range of the home radio station, then the best key was of no use anyway.

Lieutenant Commander Müller shook the thought off. It was irrelevant right now. "Heidkamp, what are the destroyers doing?"

"Still astern, throwing depth charges!"

"All four of them?"

"I hear three, the fourth must be drifting and listening!"

"Well, he doesn't hear much in that circus!"

Someone was laughing somewhere, but the noise quickly stopped. Müller looked at the IWO. "Question: runtime?"

Rothe looked at his stopwatch. "Almost gone! Ten..."

One impact interrupted him. It barely sounded like an explosion, but Müller knew that at that moment one of his torpedoes had hammered into a ship's flank. And another impact followed right after that! Sailors started to cheer, but Müller raised his hand. "Silence in the boat, men!"

The cheering stopped as quickly as it had started. The old man took a look at the depth gauge. 20 meters went through. Thank God! Thank God! The big propellers of the freighter in front of them sounded pretty damn close. But he suppressed the impulse to make Heidkamp listen forward. The destroyers, the real danger, were somewhere astern. Now, in those moments, the British escort commander would realize that he was dealing with two submarines. So what would he do?

For a moment Müller's thoughts returned to the surface. He saw in his mind's eye the glistening magnesium light of the grenades again. He hadn't expected the Limeys to fire flares, because that could lure more submarines to their convoy. Obviously, the British saw things differently. It had been a misjudgment and Müller wondered what else he had assessed differently from his British counterparts.

"Destroyer is picking up speed!" The voice of the young sailor who passed on Heidkamp's reports suddenly sounded tense and the commander knew that the man involuntarily passed on the tension of the hydrophone operator. "Second Destroyer is following!"

So the British had split up. Two remained at the first target, the other submarine, the other two came around to give U-15 hell.

The sound of the freighters above began to change slowly, and he already knew what was going on before the message came from the radio shack: "Convoy is changing course!

"Whereto?"

"Give us a moment ... Heidkamp believes to port, but is not sure yet!"

Port, that meant north! On a battlefield at sea everything is always in motion. Only the fatally wounded ships no longer moved. Since their first attack, the freighters had already covered more than six miles and even U-15 with its crawl speed had made about two miles. So the freighters turned around the position of the other submarine, not over it.

For the English on the surface it had to be tense moments. To maneuver a monster like a convoy required overview and experience. At least as far as experience went, the Limeys still lacked it. Of course, there had been occasional convoys in the past, but the British admiralty was not a friend of the convoy system. Müller smiled a little mockingly. His IIWO, Andreas Rader, could perhaps calculate exactly that the Limeys would profit from convoys, perhaps even take the edge off the just declared unrestricted submarine war before it really started, but Müller had grown up in the navy. Mathematics, logic or even common sense meant nothing until one's own admiralty was convinced. Already two years earlier British admirals had publicly mocked the insignificant effects of a submarine war and prevented the British from introducing a continuous convoy system. It wasn't a secret. Of course, there were always reasons for it and against it and they had also been discussed in the newspapers in Germany and England up to the point of public vomiting, but here and now everything came down to one simple fact: The English didn't know much about sailing in convoys and the Germans didn't have much experience in attacking escorted convoys. Everything might have looked beautiful and simple on paper, in a cozy warm room in the admiralty, but out here things were different simply because they had to be different.

"One of the freighters stops!"

This had to be the first one they had torpedoed, but Müller grimaced. Heidkamp was good, he already fished a lot out of the chaos of all those noises, but he wouldn't hear everything either. Above them the big propellers of the merchant ships were still thundering. The destroyers could Heidkamp only hear because their turbines produced a higher pitched whistling. If he could hear a single freighter, it was only because ...it was swinging around. "New course two-zero-zero!"

"Two-zero-zero, yes, Herr Kaleun!" Rader tapped the warrant officer on the shoulder. "Starboard 20!"

"LI, what's left in the batteries?"

"About three hours at this speed!"

The old man suppressed a sigh. "Turn off all unnecessary equipment, save power!"

The IWO joined him. "All tubes secured!" Rothe looked at him questioningly. "What do you think..."

"Wait and see, Herr Rothe, wait and see..." Müller waved off. "I don't think the Limeys have developed a penchant for convoying yet. There's 20 or 30 big ships up there turning now. If things come bad for them, they've got their hands full avoiding collisions!"

"You mean the Limeys don't have time to chase us now?"

The old man looked for a heartbeat quite surprised, then he shook his head. Rothe was an outstanding sailor, perhaps the best he had ever sailed with, but to become a commander, he lacked still some understanding. "Oh, no, they'll try to catch us if they can. This is the bloody Royal Navy we've invited to dance here. IIWO!" Müller looked over his shoulder. "What does your math say about the situation?"

"Three hours of power, sunrise is around six. We will have enough distance when we emerge!"

"I don't understand?" Rothe frowned. "You think the Limeys want to wait for daylight?"

Müller shrugged. "They hesitated for a long time to change the course of the convoy, didn't they? And they shot flares to see something. You see, as long as we're underwater, they can't do anything to us and they know it. To hit a submarine with depth charges, they need a lot of luck, if they can get a contact at all."

"But if they can keep us under water until we run out of power..."

"That's right, Herr Rothe..." Müller looked around and looked at the worried faces in the con. A grin appeared on his face. "Now, get a hold on yourself, men! The limeys are not smarter than we are! Nobody's saying we have to stay down till the batteries are drained. All we need is some distance and the last two hours of darkness!"

The men visibly relaxed. The old man wasn't worried, so why should they be? Müller kept the grin on his face, although it felt more like an advanced spasm to him. Of course, things were never as simple as they appeared, and the English would want to have a say in this too. What if the Limeys didn't give them a chance to surface? Up there, they had the advantage of speed. Half an hour at full speed on the surface and they were out of sight when the sun would rise. Under water, when they had to save electricity, they covered just a mile an hour and when daylight came and they had to surface, a sharp-eyed lookout might still spot them.

"Destroyer approaching!"

Müller nodded calmly. "Silence in the boat, silent running!" He looked around. "He can hardly hear us when he's running at full power! Keep calm, men!"

Minutes passed, then a higher pitch mixed with the muffled roar of the freighter propellers and the pounding of heavy machines: smaller propellers running at higher speeds. That was the first one of the two destroyers who had turned on them. Little by little they could even hear the whistling of the turbines inside the tube. The warship had to be close. Louder, louder and louder, the sound of the propellers became a racket as if a train was about to run straight over them.

He can't even hear us, how ... but Kaleun Müller gave up on the thought. Somehow the Limey destroyer had figured out where they were sneaking around. He reached for hold. Now every moment the Brit had to drop his depth charges ... now, every moment ... he had to stand already almost above them ...

But then the sound faded again as the British warship ran over the submarine and gained distance ahead. However, the respite did not last long, already the propellers of the second destroyer screamed over their heads.

The men held their breath. Now for sure! That just couldn't go well twice. But then, it did exactly that! The second destroyer wandered past their port side and then the thunder of his propellers became lower again. No dull explosions rolled through the sea, no heavy blows shook their boat ... the Limeys just sailed pass them, as if the submarine didn't even exist.

The further and further, the racing propellers faded in the distance, minutes later it was no longer audible without the hydrophone. The men waited in silence. The discipline forbade them to speak, but some still shook their heads in disbelief. Those Limeys really acted like bloody beginners?

Also Lieutenant Commander Müller was surprised. "Heidkamp?"

"They are sailing on just like nothing, away from the convoy. The first lad's heading for zero-nine-three, the other one is rather heading for zero-nine-five."

"Thank you!" The old man took off his cap and scratched the back of his head. "Well, I don't know what they're thinking either, but we lured two away from our comrades and sank at least two more freighters. Our work here is done." He spun around to the IWO. "Herr Rothe, we turn to three-one-five, slow and cozy, and sneak away."

"Back under the convoy?"

"Under the aft end through. We stay at 30 meters depth."

"Yes, Herr Kaleun!" Rothe tapped the helmsman on the shoulder. "Starboard ten! Slow and cozy, the commander said."

"Well, let's make it smooth, Herr Oberleutnant." The helmsman smirked widely. "And then let's go home! Rudder is starboard ten!"

Müller had watched the short scene in silence. They were not home yet. First they had to break away from the convoy and its escorts, then sail around Scotland and then sneak through the North Sea with its minefields before they would moor again in Wilhelmshaven. It was still a long way to go, but still… the old man shared the feeling of his men. They were on their way home.

12
Withdrawal Maneuvers

Wednesday 7 February 1917, 40 miles north of Ireland ... shortly after three o'clock in the morning.

Again, the boat had been silent. The men sat around like statues, only those who absolutely had to, moved. The air was bad, but "bad" is always a question of the standards. By the standards of the submariners, the mixture of petroleum and oil vapors, food leftovers and old socks was still quite breathable for hours to come. More worries caused the battery charge. The engineer knocked several times against the glass of his instruments. "Two hours!"

"Not three?"

"We're using more power than I thought we'd use." The lieutenant snapped his fingers and gave a sign to one of his stokers. The man set in motion on silent paws. Somewhere in the boat, something consumed a little more power than it should. Maybe a fan heater, because it was miserably cold in this damned iron tube? Maybe an auxiliary fuel pump? Or maybe they could save some power on the lamps somewhere? Every little amp counted!

Further ahead in the boat the sailors and some of the stokers who were not on watch waited. Boatswain`s mate Kern let the look slide over the squeezed gathering. When the boat was submerged, there wasn't much to do for the sailors, so they were stowed away in the bow compartment so to speak. Living ballast, and just like with water ballast, nobody told them what was going on. The war was waged in the control room. Here in the bow compartment, they'd only bear the consequences if the big heads in the control room screwed up. But that, too, was part of submarine life. Heidkamp could listen for the enemy ships and the old man could occasionally take a look through the periscope, but the rest of the crew had no idea what was going on or what the enemy looked like. Not that Kern cared. He's been on submarines since before the war. An eternity, as it sometimes seemed to him now. Things might seem crazy to anyone outside a submarine, but it was normal for him. Even the times in the safe home port appeared to him merely as unusual interruptions. Just the last homecoming had been different. His wife had looked old. Old and haggard. And his children needed new clothes, only fabric was hard to find and shoes ... Kern didn't even want to think about shoes. Everything was scarce, everything was needed for the war effort and nothing more came into the country. The English blockaded Germany almost since the first day of the war. The homeland simply ran out of steam.

Boatswain`s mate Kern did not claim to be a particularly intelligent man. He did his job conscientiously and honestly and he did his duty in a war he had not wanted. He had already been one of the few who hadn't cheered anno '14. One of the old naval men who knew the Royal Navy from fleet visits in peacetime, fleet parades and occasional simultaneous visits to ports of other nations. In the Imperial Navy, the rejoicing had been limited from the beginning, because nobody could seriously indulge in any illusions about the strength of the enemy. Nevertheless, many had not seen it as hopeless. The German High Seas Fleet was strong, on the paper about a third of the British fleets, but in reality probably a little stronger because the German battleships were better armored and the British ships were spread out around the world.

The High Seas Fleet, the High Seas Fleet, the High Seas Fleet ... Grand Admiral Tirpitz's dream, the Emperor's pride, that was all everybody had in mind. Until it turned out that the High Seas Fleet was anchored in Wilhelmshaven and could not get out.

From the first day of the war, submarines had fought against the enemy, hampered by the cruiser rules, too small and too weakly armed, and most types with too little range. U-15 had been one of these boats and not even one of the smallest or weakest. Today, of course, three years later, U-15 was outdated, didn't have enough torpedoes and the range could of course be longer, but U-15 was still sailing because Germany couldn't afford to put the old boats out of service, and just like Kern, the old boat, which was not so old in years, did its duty.

The mate's hand caressed the rusty steel. So we did it again, old girl. All the torpedoes were out! No one had told them yet, but there was no option than for the old man to leave now and sail back home. What else could he do?

A loud, long rumble ran through the water and U-15 shook slightly. Color particles rained from the ceiling. The men looked up surprised. That was close! Not dangerously close, but also not far enough away to feel safe. What the hell were they doing up there in the control room?

*

But also in the control room the men looked at each other dazzled as the explosions echoed through the water.

"What the hell..." Lieutenant Rothe was unable to bring the curse to an end. New detonations rolled through the depths. Two... three... four... then several at once! Pressure waves ran through the sea, reached U-15 and shook the boat. There was not much glass left that could break, but once again lose items flew through the iron tube and the lights flickered. Cussing, the men grabbed for hold.

It appeared to take an eternity for the thunder to finally fade away. The men looked each other in the pale faces. That had been at least 20 explosions, maybe more! The IWO was baffled. "The British destroyers don't have that many depth charges on board, do they?"

The commander bent down and picked up the cap that had dropped from his head in the confusion. "No, they don't!" He took a deep breath. "I have no idea what that was. Heidkamp, where are the boys? What are they doing?"

"That friggin' rumbling came from two-zero-zero, give or take!" Heidkamp pressed one of the earphones of the headset against the ear, ready to tear it away immediately, should the noise begin again. "Two destroyer lads in three-three-six, two others far, roughly bearing in zero-six-zero."

"Are they dropping depth charges?"

"I don't hear shit! They seem to be circling. It's hard to hear something, all the water is stirred up."

Müller blinked in consternation. None of the destroyers were even in the bearing from which the explosions had come, and none of the English warships was close enough to their U-boat to attack it, even if the Limeys would make contact. "Damage reports?"

One of the stokers came from astern: "Starboard exhaust flap makes water, short circuit in the engine electrics of Engine I."

Klempke nodded. "How bad is it?"

"Not much water and the boys are already drying the short-cut", the stoker reported. "Water and some worn insulation, that's all!"

"If we surface, can we use the number I?"

Hinze, the electric stoker, shrugged. "Give us ten minutes, Herr Kaleun."

"But no noise!"

"No noise, I promise." The man tipped at his cap and disappeared aft.

Müller looked at his chief engineer expressionlessly. "You don't want to go aft?"

"Over a cable for ten pfennigs?" Klempke shook his head. "The mates have it under control!" He made a sad face. "The insulation is no longer pre-war quality, that's all."

The old man nodded. "Yeah, everything is short, including the rubber." He hesitated for a moment. "But we still don't know who threw depth charges around."

"Those weren't depth charges at all!"

Rothe and Müller turned to Rader and the commander had to smile. "Weren't they?"

"I don't think so." The IIWO shrugged off. "Too many for one destroyer, and they sounded different, even more protracted than a long series of individual explosions."

"What do you think it was?"

Andreas Rader looked at his commander uncertainly. "You're really sure you got Maggie's drawers with the third torpedo?"

"We didn't hear any impact." Müller was thinking. "You think we hit another ship that's slowly sinking?"

"The bearing would fit, wouldn't it?"

"Yes, but…" Müller looked at the IIWO uncertainly. "There's the wish rather like the father to thought, isn't it?"

"I can't imagine what else could have blown up. Must've loaded some ammo, that guy!"

"Then there's quite a mess up there now."

"Probably…" Rader adjusted his cap a little more boldly. "The only question is, what do our comrades do now. Because they also know that the destroyers could barely keep in touch during the noise."

"You believe…"

But already torpedo impacts echoed again through the Irish Sea and gave them the answer. For a moment the officers stared at each other, then the old man nodded. "It's a bad night to be a Limey, isn't it?"

"A very bad night."

Müller turned away and looked around. "All right, silence in the boat, we'll sneak away further."

13
North Course

Wednesday, 7 February 1917, 20 miles west of Scotland … shortly after ten in the morning

The commander stood between the tower watch leaning comfortably against the parapet and smoked a cigar. Thoughtfully he looked across the gray sea. Visibility was good. Shortly after they had surfaced, at five o'clock, they had sailed through some morning fog, but the haze had dissipated. Sea state three, hardly any of the waves carried a trace of foam at all and it was miserably cold, but only a few clouds were found in the sky, so at least they would not get a snowstorm. For the old man, at the moment, life was great, and what would come tomorrow was a problem for tomorrow.

Boots clattered on the ladder and then one of the sailors slipped out of the hatch. "Radio message, Herr Kaleun!"

"Radio message? For us?"

"From U-31, Herr Kaleun!"

The skipper grinned. "Well, let's have a look then."

The sailor gave him the note and Müller browsed over the short message: "Warmest thanks for the distraction! Caught two and saw your third freighter blow up." Müller produced some little puffs of cigar smoke. "So, he saw that!" He passed the radio message to Rader, who had the watch. "Read for yourself, Herr Leutnant."

Also the IIWO skimmed over the news. "So it was an ammunition freighter!"

"You were right again."

The young sub-lieutenant looked thoughtfully out at the sea. "Yes, probably. "One ammunition freighter more or less, I wonder if that makes a difference?"

"You know what people say: Every little bit helps!" Müller briefly looked at his IIWO and then shrugged his shoulders. "It's war, we all have orders to obey and our orders are to sink ships."

Rader took a quick look around. The tower was crowded. The narrow world of a submarine left no room for doubt, not even up here. Apparently calm, he shrugged. "Well, we can do that!"

The old man grinned and put the cigar between his lips again. "Well, then, we're exactly where we belong."

But Rader knew it was all just a facade. An ammunition freighter could carry thousands of tons of ammunition, of course. Should the English combine their ships into large convoys and should the German U-boats succeed occasionally decimating such convoys effectively, then such a convoy battle could have the same effects on the war as a won battle on land. Of course, nobody was more aware of the numbers than Rader. Only at Verdun, the artillery alone had fired thousands of tons of ammunition every day. The army stood with the back to the wall and the Entente sailed around at all times with countless ships carrying everything she needed for the war. Germany was about to lose that war. Not today and not tomorrow, the carnage could still go on for a long time, but in the end the result was inevitable. If Germany failed to break the British blockade, the civilian population would starve and the armies could no longer be supplied. Germany would simply run out of steam – and a single ammunition freighter made no difference in this picture.

They had sunk three ships last night. All together maybe 100 or 150 men killed and about 10,000-15,000 tons of goods sent to the bottom of the sea. In the cold military logic this was considered a success, but just a few hundred miles from here, in Flanders, generals still quickly sacrificed a few thousand men just to test the enemy's strength in a particular section of the endless Western Front. Like everything else, men were nothing more than one of the commodities of war, without individuality, faceless, degraded to pure numbers. Andreas Rader loved numbers, they always seemed clear and somehow clean to him. But not these numbers.

They got away, but on this morning he felt weary, exhausted and disgusted, and the worst of all, he could feel that the old man felt the same behind his facade of apparent indestructibility. It was a confusing recognition for the young officer. It made the commander human and thus vulnerable in an indeterminate way, and if the commander was vulnerable ... Rader looked forward where the long foredeck pushed through the sea. It was not difficult to imagine the swarming life inside the boat. Men who crawled into the stink of their predecessors at the change of watches, because of course not everyone had his own bunk. Men who stood and sat on watch in their stations, crowded together. Men who tried to catch some sleep somewhere. Men everywhere, and they all depended on their old man being as indestructible as he, Rader, did.

*

Lieutenant Commander Müller also pondered. Not about the big war. A commander always worries first about his boat and his crew. After this patrol he would have to write an assessment about Rothe. If he judged him well, then his IWO would command his own boat in a few months. Was Rothe ready for this? Müller doubted it. Only the demands of war would hardly wait for Max Rothe to be really ready for his own command, thus he would be promoted one way or the other, not after this patrol, but after the next or the one after, and by then he would have an angry and overly ambitious IWO who would take every opportunity to show off his special leadership qualities. Such things could easily backfire.

Then there was Klempke. Klempke was an engineer, which meant that if he wanted to be promoted, he had to leave the submarines and go somewhere into a staff or be transferred to one of the capital ships that swung around their anchors in Wilhelmshaven. It would be a complete waste of Klempke's skills, but a higher rank and thus a little more pay would help him keep his family afloat. Everything became more expensive, of course, also a consequence of the blockade. Klempke had a wife, two children and a third on the way. It would be unfair to block Klempke's career just because he wanted to keep him on board, but who knew what he would get as a replacement?

That's what led his thoughts to Rader. This was the IIWO's first war patrol as a watch officer. He was reliable, intelligent, only still considerably too insecure in dealing with the men and seamanlike ... Müller lacked the words. Rothe was primarily a sailor, Rader primarily an academic, but the chances that he would actually get a real naval officer as a replacement for Rothe were slim. U-15 was an old boat and not high on the list of priorities. So maybe an uncertainty factor he knew would work out better than a lucky game with the personnel office.

The men started to stir. "What's that?"

One of the lookouts pointed to the sky. Müller recognized two dark dots that moved slowly from aft to ahead.

"Birds?"

He swallowed a sharp remark to Rader. Instead, he took a deep breath. "Those, gentlemen, are planes!"

"Planes?"

Of course everyone knew that there were airplanes, that airplanes fought over the western front, that many men had harvested considerable war glory with this new weapon and often there had been pictures in the newspapers. Only very few of the men in U-15 had ever seen one.

Rader peered at the two tiny dots. "Still a long way off, but they gotta be fast."

"Right!" Müller produced a few more puffs of smoke. "And as high as they are, they've discovered us a long time ago."

"Then why don't they attack?"

The old man suppressed the impulse to roll his eyes. "With what? With a few machine guns? They can barely sink us, and even if they have bombs..." He let his glance glide over his boat. "We're not exactly a big bloody battleship they can't miss."

"Well?"

Müller looked at Rader. "Ask below if they're transmitting... if Heidkamp can find the frequencies, that is."

"Radio... yes, Herr Kaleun!" The IIWO bent over the speaking tube and passed the request down.

Müller considered his options. He could dive, but if they had to resurface in a few hours, there would still be daylight and they would hardly stand a few miles away from their present position. The planes would be able to find them again without any problems. Or he could steer further out to sea, trying to get out of range of these curious fellows. "Herr Rader! Steer three-zero-zero-zero! Tell the master to set up a course that will lead us at least 50 miles off the coast."

"Yes… Heidkamp's on the radio."

"Thanks!"

"Port ten!" The IIWO observed the compass with hawk's eyes.

Müller took a quick look forward. Already the long bow began to swing around. Satisfied, he turned his attention back to the planes. Thoughtfully he watched the two machines. So the Limeys now used planes to patrol for submarines off their own coast. Only the British pilots had not attacked! Why not? For Müller, the answer appeared clear. Because there were warships somewhere in the vicinity. They had not attacked because they did not need to.

A moment later they heard the report from below through the speaking tube: "The Limeys are transmitting and somebody is answering somewhere north of their position." One didn't have to be a clairvoyant to know what was coming at them with maximum speed.

For a moment the two officers looked at each other in silence, then Müller nodded. "Full ahead, if you please, Herr Rader!"

"Full ahead, Herr Kaleun!" Rader's voice didn't betray anything about his feelings. The boat would run at full speed scarcely twelve knots. Considerable for a submarine, but against the 27, a destroyer or cruiser could produce, it was nothing at all. How far would a radio on an airplane reach? Certainly not as far as a ship's station, but out here, where no mountains or buildings stood in the way, it could still be 50 miles, maybe even 60. But the fact that the radio could reach that far didn't mean it had to. The ship that had responded to the planes could stand just as well right behind the horizon. The radio range of the planes limited only how far away it could be away, if they were so lucky. Rader leaned over the speaking tube: "Machines, all four full speed ahead!"

"All engines ahead full, yes, Herr Leutnant!"

It only took a moment and the men already felt the stern dig deeper into the sea as the boat picked up more speed, even before the message came out of the speaking tube: "Engines are running at full speed!

"Thank you!" He straightened up again and took a look at the two pilots who had already reported the change of course of the boat to the hunters. The planes couldn't hang out here forever, their fuel was limited. At some point they had to turn back and return to their aerodrome. Then the old man could change course again, try to sneak out of the approach direction of the English. If that didn't work ... this time the Limeys weren't hindered by a convoy, this time they could stay on the ball as long as they managed to keep a sonar contact. At some point, they would run out of battery charge and had to return to the surface. If there was still daylight at this time, the Limeys would sink the boat; if it were already night, the Germans would probably escape. The Germans knew that and the English knew it just as well. There was no fog of war, no Clausewitzian uncertainty of commanders this time, there was only the game of distances and speeds.

*

The watch changed at noon and the master took over, but the commander stayed topside. A short time later, calls announced that the two planes were finally turning away.

Sub-Lieutenant Rader sat in mess and poked listlessly around in his food. Rothe and Klempke were also silent. There wasn't much to say. Either the English would find them or not, and if they did, they would either be able to hide in the depth till darkness fell or not. Or at least that was the general view. Surprised, the officers lifted their heads when boots rumbled down the iron ladder to the control room. Already they heard the yelled report: "Tower hatch is secured!"

Klempke jumped up with a cuss as the boat began to descent almost terribly slowly forward. Rader also jumped up. He must have overheard the alarm!

But there was no hustle and bustle at the control room, no yelling of orders, just the hissing of quick-release valves. The commander stood next to the deep rudders and waved two stokers at the valves to vent the trim cells. When his officers raced through the bulkhead, he turned around calmly. "Ah, gentlemen!" He beamed at their surprise. "You didn't think your old man still knows how to dive a boat?"

Klempke came to an abrupt halt and looked at him. "No alarm?"

"No, we dive very slowly and cozily. No need to get excited." He looked at the central schema. "Call out at 20 meters!"

"But the English destroyers...?" Rothe looked at his commander in bewilderment.

"I have no idea where they are."

"We're turning back to the East?"

The old man nodded. "Finally someone's asking the right question!"

"And the right question is, where do the English expect us last?" The LI leaned against the periscope shaft. "Right where we just came from."

Müller nodded. "Well, gentlemen, while you're here: I'll go to the mess and see if you've left anything of the lunch." He did not wait for an answer, but slipped through the bulkhead.

The officers looked at each other, then Rothe smiled. "So the old man came up with a new trick to fool the Limeys again."

"They won't get him for a long time yet!"

Sub-Lieutenant Rader watched a couple of men poke each other in the ribs. The Limeys are being tricked again! It was almost as if he could hear their thoughts. But then he thought of the man who had just slipped back into the lonely mess. How did he do it? Not to keep coming up with new tricks. There were always new tricks. But how did he constantly live with the fear that today could be the day when no new one ever occurred to him?

"30 meters up!" The master nodded to the officers. "It's still my watch for the next three hours."

Shortly before four o'clock in the afternoon, Heidkamp heard several warships in the hydrophone at a great distance, but the British – and who else would it be – quickly wandered aft. Shortly before six o'clock the boat appeared dripping out of the sea and the petroleum engines started once more. At dusk His Majesty's U-15 set course north again. Another scare lived through and able to tell about. A few more days through the North Sea and then mooring in Wilhelmshaven. What could possibly go wrong now?

14
The Fisherman

Monday, February 12, 1917, 45 miles northwest of Wilhelmshaven … shortly after two in the morning

The outermost outpost boat of the chain carried officially no name, but only a number: VP556. Outpost boats, mostly fishing boats with no weapons worth mentioning, were dispensable. They stood far outside the defensive minefields in the North Sea, and sent regular reports. When they stopped broadcasting, the command knew the enemy was at sea and off their own coast. Outpost boats were expendable and didn't need names. But that was, as always, only half the truth.

In reality VP556 was a small, stocky trawler who, in more peaceful times, had made a living from herring fishing under the name Ookensiel – and now, though not in official naval records, the small boat was generally known under the nickname "The Fisherman". Because as the last boat in the line of outliers, it was the boat that was detached when ships ran on mines, or, that happened more and more, planes fell into the North Sea. These days, The Fisherman fished for survivors.

Around two o'clock in the morning the trawler steamed along the mine field, that was marked with DE-2 in the maps of the German admiralty, not far from one of the strictly secret passages through the deadly barrier, which allowed the Germans to enter Wilhelmshaven or to break out from there. The deck was blacked out, none of the men spoke. Despite the cold, they had taken off their caps to hear better. About an hour ago they had heard two dull explosions – a sound the men knew all too well: Mines. There were thousands of them out here. But after that it was quiet again. No desperate radio messages had raced through the ether, no flames had ripped a damaged ship out of the darkness and no signal rockets were calling for help. There was only silence ruling the cold night. It was a bad sign, a very bad sign.

"Quiet!" One of the men stood up on the foredeck. Then a second man. "Port side!"

The commander, a warrant officer, not even a fully commissioned officer, hesitated only a moment before he swung the wheel around. "Ahead slow, Otto!"

The sailor he had spoken to rang the command through to the only machinist aft in the tiny engine room. While the fishing boat was still turning, it lost speed, just in time, because the minefield was on their port side. At home, in the safe chart room, these barriers looked like large rectangles, precise, as if drawn with a ruler, but out here in the North Sea you never knew exactly. No ship's position was so accurate, not in the darkest night, not when all the beacons were extinguished and all the buoys pulled in for the duration of the war. The edge of the minefield might still be 100 meters away, or 50 – or perhaps the outermost row was already lurking under the keel. But none of the sailors protested or even hesitated ... because they had heard something!

It still took a few minutes for them to find the men. The two strongest sailors of the crew hung on both sides of the recovery net, grabbed the castaways out of the water and handed them up to two other comrades on deck. It was a maneuver in which the men, unfortunately, already had way too much practice.

There were only three, one of them an officer. The warrant officer who commanded VP556 came out onto the deck and crouched next to one of the saved sailors. "What happened?"

The still young officer stared at him in the darkness and the warrant officer could hear his teeth clatter from the cold. "My boat, U-15, ran into a mine around 1:00. We were on watch duty..." The man fell silent.

The commander of the outpost boat looked at his mate. "Take them under deck. I'll sail another round, or two!"

One or two rounds became several search circles, but of course the submarine was not exactly where they had found the men. Men on the surface of the sea drift off, submarines on the bottom of the sea don't, and of course, unless someone or something from the sunken boat came up to the surface, they could sail right over the wreck and would not notice a thing.

Only in the morning, when the sun was already in the sky and there were no more survivors to expect, did The Fisherman return to his position to be relieved a few hours later by another outpost boat. Around noon The Fisherman moored at the pier and Sub-Lieutenant Rader, boatswain`s mate Kern and Seaman Müller were taken by an ambulance to the hospital. There were no other survivors of U-15.

Months later, during the investigation of another ship's loss not far from the sinking position of U-15, it was discovered that many of the mines that had been laid in 1914 had been moved over time by currents, by the sea, maybe by storms, but moved nevertheless. Only by the time, this was discovered, two other U-boats were already missing in that area.

Hindsight

In the spring of 1917, the German Reich proclaimed the unrestricted U-boat War – for the second time in this war. The first time after the sinking of the Lusitania, Germany had returned to war according to the cruiser rules, but not this time.

In fact, the unrestricted submarine war was a desperate measure. England's blockade had stopped any trade by sea, Germany suffered hunger. The last attempt to break the British blockade had failed in the summer of 1916 in the Battle of Jutland. It had been a German victory, but it wasn't a decisive victory and it had not weakened the Royal Navy so much that they would be forced to end the blockade. The submarine war was the attempt to pay England out with their own coin and to try to starve England to death before Germany itself ran out of supplies. The plan was illusory because the Imperial Navy did not have a sufficient number of large and modern boats to effectively decimate the British shipping, not even before the introduction of a convoy system.

It was a rather unreal situation due to the technical conditions. The submarines had not yet matured to the weapon they would be a war later. More German submarines were lost due to technical problems than due to British submarine defense measures. Conversely, England did not yet have active sonar detection like the famous ASDIC from World War II. The depth charge was a new weapon that was considered highly promising, but in fact only two submarines were damaged by depth charges during the entire first World War.

Much has been written about the British admiralty's long refusal to introduce a convoy system and about the fact that, after the admirals were forced to do so, this convoy system took the edge of the submarine war. The truth was, England did not have the weapons to effectively protect convoys. The then common method of hunting submarines was to keep them under water until they ran out of power and air and had to come to the surface, where the British destroyers and cruisers, who often took part in the submarine hunt, could sink them with their superior artillery.

This tactic was logically hardly applicable when the warships were hampered by a convoy of slow merchantmen, they had to protect. Modern historians criticize British admirals, who in 1917 had still mocked the insignificant effects of a submarine war. But that is of course all retrospection and filtered by our current knowledge and perception. At that time, the impact was not insignificant. 5,000 merchant ships went to the bottom of the sea, in the Atlantic, in the Mediterranean and in the Black Sea. It was a massacre… but it wasn't a massacre decisive for the war. Even before the introduction of a convoy system, German U-boats were never able to sink more merchant ships than England could build. In fact, the submarine war was painful for the English, but it was not of essential importance, and it eventually led to the entry of the USA into the war. If you look at the bottom line, England was the big winner of the submarine war, not only because it survived it, but even because it profited from it. The submarine war brought the neutrals closer to England's side; it led neutrals enter the war on the Entente's side and made England's occasional violations of international law acceptable. By February 1st of 1917, the German Empire had handed England something like a carte blanche.

Germany lost World War I, this defeat shapes our picture of history. But as always, that's only half the truth. Unnoticed by many modern historians, something happened in Germany at that time. A new generation of naval officers grew up in the submarine weapon and recognized its potential.

Three significant new weapons appeared on the battlefields during the first World War: Planes, tanks and submarines. Actually none was really new. Steerable balloons, armored carriages and muscle-powered submarines had already been used in the American Civil War, less than 50 years earlier. What the Great World War brought about was the logical evolution in technical and tactical terms, but hardly anyone recognized that this evolution was already bearing the seed for the next step. When the World War ended, Germany had both the technical experience and the men who knew how to use such weapons. None of these three weapons was really a German invention, but hardly anyone had as much experience as the Germans with them – on the receiving end of the carnage. At the end of the lost war, there could hardly be any doubt as to what Germany would offer if there ever were to be another conflict: Tanks, planes… and submarines!

Finally, some sentences about the submarine from this book: In order to be able to tell this fictitious story against a real background, the author borrowed the boat's name SM U-15 for his fictional crew. The real U-15 was lost already in August 1914 as the first German submarine of the war, after she had to stop due to engine troubles off the Shetlands. While the crew was still trying to repair the engine, the boat was discovered by HMS Birmingham. Hampered by thick fog, the British light cruiser missed with his artillery and, to stop an emergency dive, rammed U-15. All hands went down with the boat.

Glossary

Blue Max: Nickname for the Pour le Mérite, a Prussian order of merit. It was of blue color, and the first soldier, who was rewarded with one in World War I, was Max Immelmann; therefore Blue Max.

Comrade: This was a hard one for us. In the German military the term "Kamerad" (plural = "Kameraden") is commonly used to address fellow soldiers, at the same time communists and social democrats call themselves "Genosse" in German. In English there only is this one word "comrade", and it often has a communistic touch. I guess a US-soldier would not call his fellow soldiers "comrade"? Since the word "Kamerad" is very, very common in the German military we decided to translate it with "comrade", but do not intend a communistic meaning.

Dez: Old nautical measuring unit for measuring angles. 1 Dez = 10 degree.

Frog: Slur name for the French, in German often the term "Froschfresser" (= "frog-eater") is used too.

Hans and Franz: German saying meaning every normal guy

Herr: Mister (German soldiers address sex AND rank, meaning they would say "Mister sergeant" instead of "sergeant")

High Seas Fleet: German main battle fleet in World War 1

Kaleun: Short form for "Kapitänleutnant", which is the German rank for lieutenant commander.

Kaputt: German term extensively used in the German language meaning "broken" and/or "dead".

LI: Short for Leitender Ingenieur, meaning chief engineer

Limey: Slur name for British sailors. It originated in the American English language, but in World War I it was used by Germans as well.

Lusitania: British ocean liner that was sunk by German U-20 in 1915, after Germany had declared unrestricted submarine warfare for the first time. Among the 1.198, who died in the incident, were 128 US citizens, which led to harsh protests by Washington that finally ended the first period of unrestricted submarine warfare.

Merchant raider: Merchant ship that has been converted into a warship. German merchant raiders often used their civil appearance to ambush enemy ships. Technically, by the words of the cruiser rules, merchant raiders or just raiders were auxiliary cruisers for which the same rules applied as for British auxiliary cruisers.

Müller: One of the most common German surnames, which explains why there are two Müllers on U-15.

Old Man: In German military language the "Alte" (= "old man") is a common term used by lower ranks when talking about their company leader or commander without him being present. The English equivalent is "skipper" for commanders in the navy.

Sir: Obviously Germans do not say "Sir", but that was the closest thing we could do to substitute a polite form that exists in the German language. There is no match for that in the English language: In German parts of a sentence changes when using the polite form. If one asks for a light in German, one would say "Hast du Feuer?" to a friend, but "Haben Sie Feuer?" to a stranger or any person one have not agreed with to leave away the polite form yet. During the Second World War the German polite form was commonly spread, in very conservative families children had to use the polite form to address their parents and even some couples used it amongst them. Today the polite form slowly is vanishing, like the capital spelled form of "You" in English as well. Some companies like Ikea even addresses customers informally in the first place – something that was an absolute no-go 50 years ago.

SM (as a ship's prefix): Stands for "His Majesty's" (= "Seiner Majestät") SMS was in the time of the German Imperial Navy an equivalent prefix for the British HMS and the American USS.

VP-boat: Because the number of German warships was very limited in World War I, the Imperial Navy modified a lot of small civil craft for military purposes. Those so-called VP-boats (short for "Vorpostenboot" meaning outpost boat) were used to guard coastal areas.

Watch Officer: With each German WWI submarine crew came two watch officers, the 1st Watch Officer (IWO) and the 2nd Watch Officer (IIWO). They were the second respectively the third officer on board after the commander.

About the Author

Peter Brendt, born in 1964, joined the German Navy after Abitur (which is equivalent to high school graduation). He attended training as a navigator and later as a weapons diver. Terms of service were predominantly spent in NATO commands. Following his resignation from the Navy, he studied business and computer sciences. Since 2005, Brendt earns his living as a full-time author. He is married and lives in the U.S. with his wife, writer Diane Brendt.

Your Satisfaction Is Our Goal!

Dear Reader,

We hope you enjoyed this book. Do you have any comments, criticism or ideas for books you want to read in the future? Please do not hesitate to contact us. We read every Email personally and answer it as soon as possible. Your opinion is of great value for us.

Contact us: info@ek2-publishing.com

You can help us to keep history alive by taking a moment's time to review this book on Amazon. Many positive reviews lead to more visibility for our books. A few words or a simple star review help our authors and our publishing company to increase our quality with every book published. Thank you for your support!

PS: In rare case scenarios a book might get damaged during shipment. If that should be the case, please do not hesitate to contact us and we will replace the book at no charge.

Your EK-2 Publishing Team
The publisher close to its readers

Our recommendations for you!

Iron Cross – Never Surrender!
Book 1
By Tom Zola

In November 1942, Hitler dies in a plane crash. The Nazi Party collapses, and the German military takes over. Facing defeat, they launch a last-ditch panzer offensive at Kursk to stop the advancing Soviets.

Shingas
By Barry Cole

»Shingas« tells the tragic tale of the fight between the Iroquois tribe and the overpowering British troops. Especially the warrior Shingas battles them with merciless brutality. Experience the conquest of the American East through the eyes of this fearless warrior.

Available on all major platforms!

Published by EK-2 Publishing GmbH

Friedensstraße 12
47228 Duisburg - Germany
Register court: Duisburg - Germany
Company registration number: HRB 30321
CEO: Monika Münstermann

E-Mail: info@ek2-publishing.com
Website: www.ek2-publishing.com

Cover art: Mario Heyer
Author: Peter Brendt
Translation & Editing: Jill Marc Münstermann
Layout: Eduard Krisan

1. edition, May 2025

Printed in Great Britain
by Amazon

62724444R00058